HARD TO FIND:

An Anthology of New Southern Gothic

HARD TO FIND:

An Anthology of New Southern Gothic

edited by

Meredith Janning

with a foreword by

Joe R. Lansdale

STEPHEN F. AUSTIN STATE UNIVERSITY PRESS

For more information:
Stephen F. Austin State University Press
P.O. Box 13007 SFA Station
Nacogdoches, Texas 75962
sfapress@sfasu.edu
www.sfasu.edu/sfapress

Managing Editor: Kimberly Verhines
Book Design: Meredith Janning
Cover Design: Meredith Janning
Cover Art: Peering Out (ink, dust, and glue on found photograph) by Julie Blankenship. Instagram @privateyesf; Facebook: Julie Blankenship

Distributed by Texas A&M Consortium
www.tamupress.com

ISBN: 978-1-62288-945-7

For my family,
who instilled in me a love of stories

CONTENTS

Editor's Note

IN ITS OWN WAY, the American South is riddled with elements of the gothic genre. Instead of empty, isolated castles it has small towns, though just as haunted, just as full of secrets. The Southern Gothic is a clash between the old and the new, tradition and breaking the cycles its people are ashamed of. It's grotesque and violent, surreal and symbolic but it makes people listen. It's about calling people to change or be forgotten. In the past, this genre had writers like Flannery O'Connor, William Faulkner, Carson McCullers, Tennessee Williams—the list goes on—but these ideas and experiences are just as present today as they ever were.

Hard To Find: An Anthology of New Southern Gothic was born out of questions I had about the state of Southern Gothic fiction today. Among them, I asked: how do you define the South? What makes Southern people different? Has anything really, truly changed from its history? Compelled to find an answer, I decided to create, with the Stephen F. Austin State University Press, an open submission call for an anthology that would house new entries of this genre.

It was a difficult process to determine which stories to include because the submissions were all truly devoted to the genre, but the following ten stories come from all over the country, some have even been published abroad, but they all strive and succeed to find their place in the lexicon of Southern Gothic fiction.

As editor of *Hard To Find: An Anthology of New Southern Gothic,* I hope you enjoy these stories. I know I did.

Foreword

It's The Stories
Joe R. Lansdale

First and foremost, these are good stories, and that is the most important thing to know. The wealth of a story should not be judged by its label, chosen, given, or otherwise.

The definition of Southern Gothic, which is how these stories are presented, is fun to play with in an academic way, but the truth of the matter is, stories need not necessarily belong to a club.

Southern Gothic.

Splatterpunk.

Beat.

Cyberpunk.

Gonzo.

Bizarro.

These are among the many labels good and bad stories have traveled under on their trips across magazine, book, and now internet pages.

Like escargot, they are traveling under an assumed name. Escargot, no matter how often you repeat that moniker, we all know what it really is.

Snails.

That doesn't sound appetizing, but if you have ever had snails prepared with butter, presented just right, they are amazing. These stories are properly prepared, lathered with creative butter, sometimes coating what would otherwise be unappetizing.

As Charlie Parker, better known as the "Bird" said about his love of country music, "It's the stories, man, it's the stories."

We will call these stories neither snail nor escargot, but what is clear is they wear the lanyard of Southern Gothic dangling around their necks. Beneath the lanyard is the skin, blood and bones of all good fiction.

No matter what clubhouse you assign stories too, the key you are given to the clubhouse is the same key that belongs to all writers, wearing their variety of lanyards and entering into the fiction house through different doors. Once inside, the writers and their labels mix and mingle.

Just for the record, let's talk about that group who have come through a specific door and have been given their lanyard with Southern Gothic printed on it. Let's play academic for a few moments, keeping in mind my academic credentials are a high school diploma and a few college courses, along with an over fifty-year career of writing and publishing in a variety of places under a variety of labels given to me by others.

Southern gothic is a term applied to fiction that takes place in the Southern portion of the United States and is often about characters with personal flaws, unconventional or troubling view points and actions. Violence, along with an air of decay, are also components, and sometimes there is the added spice of the supernatural. Southern Gothic characters are often on the bottom of the social scale, poor, and may even be criminal. Racism and poverty are often backbeats, or in some cases, the beats are well settled in the front row. Southern Gothic is sometimes thought to be a kissing cousin of noir.

And then, there are stories that bear the name Southern Gothic, but have a different set of ingredients than those I listed, while still providing the reader with the gothic experience.

If it sounds as if I'm struggling to define Southern Gothic, it's because it is hard to define, and finally, unnecessary.

These good stories mix and match those elements and add new ones to the pile. More contemporary ones.

Call them Southern Gothic, or whatever designation suits you, but remember this, and this is the most important rule as a writer and a reader. A good story should grab the reader. Hold them. Make them feel, and when they put the story away, the author can only hope that it leaves an echo that reverberates through the readers bones. The plot may even be forgotten, but what should not be forgotten, is how the story makes you feel.

I have a feeling after reading this collection you will experience a variety of satisfying echoes.

"It's the stories, man, the stories."

Enjoy.

TALLULAH

John Michael Flynn
Previously Appeared in *StylusLit*, Australia 2022

THE WISE AMONG US KNOW there are no rights. There are merely adjudications. This was Haroon Feisal Mohamed's thought as he labored to steer Jumbo Cousins' red van. Jumbo had insisted Haroon drive, and that they avoid Greenville and Hendersonville, opting instead for Route 23 North through Tallulah Falls and the gorge there. They'd then cross the Georgia state line into Waynesville and then drive Route 40 home to Asheville. Why? Because Haroon had to conquer his fear of Tallulah Gorge.

"You address it," said Jumbo. "That's how a fear is cauterized. Otherwise, it grows like a cancer."

The van didn't feature power steering. Its wheel vibrated, torqueing to one side. Jumbo's vehicle, all right, one of a kind, thought Haroon. The man was persuasive, hard to control, idiosyncratic, fearless, with no quit in him. One who understood adjudications.

Jumbo had explained: "I'm doing this for you. I don't just let anybody drive my van. You need to get through that gorge on your own. It's the only way."

This brought no comfort to red-eyed Haroon, the van the only sign of motion on the unlit narrow and twisting ribbon of asphalt. Haroon was spent. They'd stood for the entire concert at Atlanta's Fox Theatre, having been lucky to get in.

Jumbo had been persuasive. "Farewell tour, post-pandemic, time to get out and live. It's once in a lifetime, Haroon, and a Friday night, and I can get standing-room-only tickets. They're not cheap, but I'll pay for yours. I know you're a big fan, Haroon. Their music. Our generation. I'd feel like we missed out if we didn't take advantage."

Haroon had agreed, though as much as he'd loved the music and appreciated a free ticket, he didn't like choosing to live based on a fear of missing out. This struck him as such an American hang-up. Yet he was an American now, fully legal after what he often jokingly referred to as his green-card years in limbo. Jumbo was right, too, about facing his fear of driving the gorge. The time had come. First the gorge, then maybe he'd summon the confidence to ask Brianna, one of his co-workers, out for a date.

Jumbo had said, "Imagine a gun pointed at your skull. How do you react? If it were me, I'd picture myself calm and full of poise. That's how you need to come across with Brianna."

Long drives. Too much time to think. Drained of the adrenalin that had made the trip from Asheville to Atlanta tolerable after a day of work, they'd stopped for supper at a Denny's. They'd wisely avoided alcohol. This had helped Haroon to navigate the van through Atlanta traffic. Once beyond city limits, he'd expected to relinquish the wheel, but Jumbo had shocked him, demanding he drive.

"You're going the distance through the gorge at night all the way up to Franklin and on over to Asheville. Now pull over so I can catch some shut-eye in the back."

The big man was still asleep. His occasional snores filled the van. Haroon kept both passenger and driver side windows open. A damp chill breezed in to keep him awake.

Was it in darkness where God began or ended? The question intrigued Haroon as he leaned forward over the dash, eying the unlit road, the air perfumed with a mingling of lush greenery and a fetid odor of earthen rot. If God came in the night, it was to express nature as a condensing dew that Haroon could taste against his teeth. There was an eeriness to the night's shine that had settled in with a severity that reminded Haroon of the obsidian gleam in a sheared lump of coal. God was a black man. Black as that fine coal.

No way he'd wake Jumbo or pull over, though the urge was strong when he felt a prickling of sweat beetle up his neck. Headlights filled his rearview mirror. They slowed when he slowed. Swerved when he swerved. There was a possum to avoid, and this nocturnal creature startled Haroon, darting across the road. Swerving again, nearly losing control of the van, Haroon thought he could hear one of the waterfalls, there were six of them, that gave the town its name. The road cut left and then right. Then right again. All the while, the waterfalls murmured out of the darkness and headlights stayed in the same place in his rearview, keeping the same distance, moving with him at the same speed. He was immersed in the gorge now, meeting Jumbo's challenge that he "get in over his head and out of his comfort zone."

The waterfalls blended with the purling of streams and Haroon thought it's not a road, it's an experience, each turn more severe than the last. At times the asphalt looked like a frayed shoelace blurred along its edges by banks of mist, crowded overhead by the effulgence of tree cover, dank vines, branches that drooped down on both sides of him. In some areas they formed a canopy that gave Haroon the feeling he was rolling through a tunnel of loamy aromatic mists.

He'd learned from Jumbo that locals had mistakenly translated the word Tallulah from Cherokee to mean "loud waters." During their supper at Denny's, Jumbo had explained that the word could have been from Choctaw, not Cherokee, but it was most likely from Creek and meant "small town with one hill." Jumbo had some Choctaw blood in him on his father's side and an abiding interest in what he called "America's buried genocidal history." Did Haroon know that of all the American tribes only the Cherokee were able to compile a dictionary of their own language? Like the Choctaw, they were removed, Trail of Tears and all that, but Haroon knew that, didn't he?

"Stick with me, Haroon, and you'll know more than most about this nation's history and it'll tear your heart out."

Haroon swerved to avoid a rut, the van racing down a steep curve that ended with an abrupt jolting turn back to the left. No margin for error. Those headlights were still there. The van wobbled, its wheel tugging and Haroon felt a shiver of panic. He didn't like being followed. Why didn't those lights back off?

He should wake up Jumbo, but that would mean surrender, and Jumbo would be angry and disappointed. So would he. Those insistent headlights weren't going to stop him. True, they made him nervous, but what was he afraid of, after all?

He knew what. Jumbo knew too, but they hadn't discussed it. A moment of relief came to Haroon as he saw the vehicle behind him was, as he'd suspected, a police car. The two beacons atop its roof were now lighting up the darkness. No siren, just a blue wash pulsing like summer lightning against the soft drapery of foliage.

Haroon stopped in the middle of the road, the one he feared. The gorge he feared. Tallulah. Like the old actress Tallulah Bankhead who Jumbo had said was named after her grandmother who'd been named after the falls. "Probably a load of Hollywood hogwash."

The big man had ceased snoring. Wake him? A second police car had arrived. From where and how so quickly, Haroon couldn't say. As if materializing out of the darkness, it was parked crossways in front of the van and blocked passage.

Haroon felt hemmed in as he shut the van engine off. The night silence with its ever-present rippling of falling water felt strangely soothing as the blue strobes kept pumping. Haroon looked out his window, squinting to see a sliver of sky above the road as if he'd entered a vast planetarium. This was a dream and he'd awakened not as intruder but as tourist, adventurer, citizen. He'd done nothing wrong. He belonged here.

What shocked him most was that he didn't feel afraid. It had to be the distant sound of water. Closing his eyes, he heard it rising up the steeps within the gorge. He breathed what smelled for a tart moment like honeysuckle, a scent he could identify. It cleaved through the ranker, more humid succulence of swamp vegetation. Rains, it seemed, had passed through here not long ago.

Crickets and chiggers and cicadas were suddenly deafening, sounding their fricative symphony in a cataract that proved this was never a quiet place. It was a tangle, a cacophony of sounds, looming walls and slithering tapestries of them. A mosquito buzzed toward his ear lobe and Haroon swiped it away and saw blood on his fingers just as he saw four cops emerging toward him from out of the darkness.

Four of them. All white men about the same age and height. They looked like mannequins of cops, their faces too clean, their eyes too small. An unnatural rigidity to their posture, two of them bulky, their blonde hair cut short, a paranoid aura about them. The other two, leaner, both with dark hair, stood back, hands ready on their belts. This was their road, their chorus of cicadas, their waterfall, their night. Haroon, facing them, understood, indeed, what he had feared. Not the gorge's natural, nocturnal breath, but its manmade one.

What should he say? He had little experience in such matters. His words should be simple, spoken softly, deferentially. He had a university education. A good job with an IT firm, and he'd worked from home during the Covid lockdown. Without telling them, the cops should sense he was a professional from the way he behaved. He knew he'd be asked for his driver's license, and the van's registration, which Jumbo kept clipped to the sun visor. He remembered that a possum played dead to avoid predators. Then he heard a robotic voice, "License and registration please."

It brought him back to many a conversation with Jumbo, who'd served tours abroad in the US Army, had experience when it came to men showing their primacy in volatile situations. Jumbo, his first and dearest American friend, a man who'd lived and served in the Middle East, had sought to understand what imperialist greed had done to many innocent people in that part of the world. "Be an open book," Jumbo liked to say. "And you'll really scare people."

Though the cop held a light pointed into Haroon's eyes, he didn't cast its beam deeper inside the van. If so, he would have seen Jumbo, who was no longer snoring. Haroon handed over his license and the registration. He'd be fine. This wasn't Jim Crow or the KKK times he'd read about. Or was it?

Now came the fear. One he knew a black man lived with daily in many a nation. You just never knew with white people. Jumbo was an oddball, an exception, an outcast in his own family. There were few like him, so generous, willing to question the status quo, each political event, regardless of the race or creed of those involved.

Haroon knew he'd been driving the speed limit, but he also knew this didn't matter. These cops had absolute power. They could do as they pleased, toying with him, even though he'd done nothing wrong.

Rights and justice, thought Haroon, were absurdly idealistic conceits. How scared he felt. There it was. It was their county, not his, no matter his passport. But he wasn't a gangster, nor would he want to be. He paid taxes and his job as a software designer had a connection to making life better for people. So, he'd been to a concert in Atlanta. Stood up in the back. Cheered over the spectacle of it all. Not a crime. Especially after the pandemic. He should remember advice Jumbo had once shared: "Don't expect. Because the surprise is always better when it comes."

Haroon felt conflicted about involving Jumbo. Daytime or night, drunk or sober, the man had driven this gorge many times. A force of nature with a philosophical bent, he had generational roots that ran deep in these parts and much wisdom when it came to what he called "the back-assward hillbilly redneck trash, my own kin, that breed hellfire out of these hills."

Let Jumbo sleep. This was his problem, his fear. Those cops didn't need to know Jumbo was back there. He'd handle this on his own. His fear, as it related to police brutality, wasn't absurd. There was the George Floyd case, and many other examples of violence and racism. Regardless of his education, or being an Egyptian-American, he was just another black man in the South, one who hadn't been born there and he had every right to quake in his shoes. Only an ignoramus wouldn't be afraid. Haroon believed Jumbo would agree with him on that point.

He was biting his lower lip when he heard, "Please, Sir, step outside the van."

The cop lowered his light beam. Imposing, but not aggressive or rude, not at all, he was polite to an extreme. So damn polite! Haroon didn't speak as he exited the van. Both shoes on the ground, arms pinned to his sides, he stood at attention telling himself not to move in any sudden manner. The test was on. He must pass. He'd pay a speeding ticket if need be. The point was to address his fear. Man up. He wasn't a native. They were. This was not his land nor his freedom, and it had never been guaranteed. Get his mind right. Shut up and listen.

Still courteous, the cop said, "Please, Sir, palms against the front end of the van and spread both of your legs."

The three other cops gathered around, and Haroon thought of them as dogs taking turns as they sniffed at and sized him up with an interest that suggested they'd never seen a man like him before. The legs of his trousers were frisked by all the cops, each one overly deliberate in the way he patted around Haroon's buttocks and under his crotch and arms. Thorough yet stiff and altogether too serious. The front of the van felt hot against Haroon's open hands. The smell of radiator fluid and motor oil torched his nostrils. One cop took his wrist and Haroon felt ice immediately in the man's grip as he led him to the police car. "Okay, Sir, get on in."

The blue strobes stopped flashing. The night seemed to rise with an intensity that matched the cicadas, a sweeping wave of sound that increased in volume. It struck Haroon that these cops weren't human.

The way they moved, disjointed, tense, showed they were brimming with fear. Shouldn't he be the one afraid?

The police car drove off ever so smoothly. Maybe, thought Haroon, he'd been wrong not to say that Jumbo was in the van. Yet sometimes taking no action was the best choice. Were these cops racist? Did his skin make him a felon? These questions lingered as Haroon sweated silently thinking of Jumbo as he swiveled his head around to see the van grow smaller.

Those cops still had his license, but they hadn't put him in handcuffs. One police car and two men were still back there and Haroon wondered if they'd search the van, wake Jumbo and poke him into roaring like a bear stirred from hibernation.

As the drive went on, Haroon felt his head dropping. He lacked the energy to stop it, drifting into a half-conscious state as he thought he heard one cop remark, "I'll wire into Rabun County." He heard the other reply, "Tell him center of Clayton, near the gorge."

They spoke in clipped cadences with so little emotion. They could take him anywhere. Who would know? No doubt all sorts of crimes had been committed on this road under cover of darkness. Haroon thought he could hear the screams. Rapes, lynchings, tribal wars, blood oozing out of the tree bark. God had, indeed, gone into hiding, but would God rise at dawn in the East? Back home, the place he'd abandoned, his father would say, "All praise Allah. But not those who know him."

This was his last thought as he fell asleep. When he awoke, he found himself seated on a metal stool inside a harshly lit room and he thought he heard someone say "sheriff's office" after a phone rang. He wasn't sure of his whereabouts. A police station. Its own little universe. The light blaring. The sounds and sensations distant and hazy. He felt as if he'd been drugged. What time was it and how long had he been in this place?

He was coaxed to stand and then locked into a cage enclosure made of heavy steel. A cop stuck a hose through a gap between the bars. Fluorescent lights glared overhead. Everything looked yellow. In the room's bright light, Haroon could see this cop was just a boy. What did he know of life? A gun on his belt. So much power.

Haroon, his mouth dry, took his end of the hose. He thought of all the poor kids in cities across the world, especially those from minority populations, whether guilty or not, who never got lessons from their fathers or friends, who never listened, who joined gangs, who lived as if they were gangsters believing they'd never get caught or fall on hard times. Until hard times came. Until one mistake was made that changed everything. Until one gang member mouthed off or showed disrespect toward the wrong person at the wrong time.

Whether in Cairo or California, the mistake was always to be ignorant. To believe you were new or original and the past didn't haunt every street, alley and building around you. It took so little to send any cop, already tense, over the edge. Even the best ones, no matter their race, could snap due to pressures of the job. The world they faced each day was rife with criminals. No one in it could be trusted. Kids, especially boys, again no matter the race, needed to be taught to understand this. Rights are not legislated. Or given out. At times, they're not even earned.

The tube in his mouth, Haroon breathed per the cop's orders while watching him read a meter at the base of a machine. There was hissing from a pipe shaped like a thin test tube. The cop assessed the meter, pressed a few buttons, and then walked away.

Where was Jumbo? What time was it? None of this was legal, was it? Enjoy the surprise. A sullen Haroon heard the big man's stentorian voice before he saw him. It was an alluring voice that carried between the station's glazed block walls, Jumbo lilting casually from side to side, entering the station with a cop stiff as a bookend on each of his arms.

Haroon felt his face burning with shame.

A born salesman, though he'd worked for years in agriculture with his hands, Jumbo now sold plumbing supplies at wholesale rates to retailers and developers. He liked to denigrate himself by saying he sold toilets for a living. During the pandemic, he'd filled orders and assured deliveries from his home. He had a baritone's voice, an easy delivery as he said no, they hadn't been drinking and that Haroon was bone tired. They both were.

Jumbo appeared so composed. As if this was normal and he did it all the time. He was manning up, finding his center, keeping the fire there on a low simmer. Identifying his outrage and compartmentalizing it. The man had skills, confidence, and a chameleon's ability to alter his persona to adapt to any situation. These were traits Haroon envied.

When Jumbo approached Haroon and sized him up, he didn't look angry. Haroon didn't believe it. Jumbo was just being kind. The man was too savvy to let his real feelings show in front of cops. Maybe he would later, in private. Haroon hoped he'd do so in a fraternal way so to teach, to build Haroon's confidence, to show forgiveness. This was a form of manning up too.

Haroon knew he looked pitiful and confused. He felt awful. Jumbo didn't respond when he muttered about the road, his fatigue.

"Why didn't you wake me?" asked Jumbo.

Haroon wanted to shrug, but he didn't. Better to speak the truth. "The gorge. My challenge. I wanted to do it myself."

Jumbo, reflecting, rubbed his chin. He and a pair of cops faced Haroon on the other side of the cage's bars. Jumbo then turned to one of the cops. "Contact Macon County, or the police station in Franklin if you want to verify anything. You can ask for the police chief. They all know my kin in those parts."

Haroon's throat was still so dry that his voice cracked when he spoke, lacking any power. "I was doing my best. Your van, it's not so easy to drive."

"Hey, hey, don't worry. You did it. You got through the gorge. I'll get us out of here." He turned to one cop, "You think my friend here can get some water?"

The cop nodded and hurried off, returning promptly with a paper cup of tap water. As Haroon sat there drinking, what frightened him most was realizing how genuinely confused and young the cops appeared. It was as if they didn't really know what they were doing and were making it up as they went along. One of the cops just gaped at him and Haroon wanted to lash out and ask why he was staring, hadn't he ever seen an Egyptian in the zoo before.

After clearing his throat, one of the cops said, "We shouldn't let him go."

"Test results first," said another cop. "We got bigger fish to fry."

"No, we don't. He's right here. We got him."

Were they arguing? It appeared so. The argument ceased when another cop, an older one built like a wrestler without a neck, as if his head had been jammed between his shoulders, became one more uniform among what was now a trio. The primary difference in the features of this third cop was that his face showed more wrinkles, his jowls giving him a bulldog's look.

Haroon found the silence unbearable. Still seated in his cage, he looked at Jumbo and saw glimpses in his friend, too, of anguished shock, despair and befuddlement.

Seasoned authority figures were less threatening than incompetent ones. Haroon blew a sigh. The bulldog cop was now, unquestionably, in charge of the situation. Feet spread, both hands on his gun belt, he assessed Jumbo, who stood at his side. He drew his eyes down and then up, needing to crane his neck because Jumbo towered over him.

Haroon was still in the gorge. Still being tested. As he waited, he could hear the falling water and he imagined moss-covered stones under foamy rills and pools of water. At last, a fourth cop appeared with the breathalyzer results. Haroon had passed. The bulldog told the others to return to their duties. He told Jumbo there'd be no charges pressed.

"Do you think you can let him out of his chicken coop?"

"You trying to be funny?" asked the bulldog cop. "I can put you in there, if you prefer."

Jumbo silenced himself. Haroon felt hopeful as he stood, waiting, and the bulldog unlocked the cage and said to him, "If I see you and your friend back here this way again, I reckon you'll regret it, you hear?"

Jumbo stepped in. "It's not gonna happen."

"That so?" The bulldog didn't appear convinced. "And I will make that call up to Macon County, and to the police chief there, you can be sure of that."

He can still hurt us, thought Haroon. They can always hurt us. "Sir, I'm very sorry."

The bulldog, unmoved, remained taciturn.

"Can he get his license back?" asked Jumbo.

"At the front desk."

Jumbo grabbed Haroon by the wrist and led him out. They retrieved the license and registration and once under the night sky, which was brightening now in the east, Haroon realized how bottled-up he'd been, burning inside. He stood a moment and tasted the air, but it wasn't sweet, and it didn't relax him. He saw a circle of cops surrounding him, their guns raised, he and Jumbo and the van in the circle's center. All the cops where white, the same build, their feet spread, their guns out and supported by two hands. He heard one of them shout, "You made it out. So now what are you gonna do?"

God, it seemed, had come out of hiding. As he got into the van, on the passenger side, Haroon said to Jumbo, "Is this really happening?"

Jumbo pursed his lips and stared straight ahead, both his big hands dangling over the steering wheel. "We got ourselves a dose of the old-school South, didn't we? Just what I was fearing, I think, more than you were." He blinked his brown eyes twice. He turned to Haroon. "Gets heightened when so much is on the line, doesn't it?"

Haroon nodded. "Once was enough. I don't have to do it again."

Jumbo sounded a sardonic, "I wouldn't let you."

They drove a long time without speaking. Haroon nodded off, waking when Jumbo decided to stop for coffee. As the morning continued to rise, they began to talk with more intensity about how fears take on various forms and play all sorts of dramas inside one's head. Haroon wanted to tell Jumbo about his hallucination, all those armed cops encircling them, but its power shrunk in his mind the more he thought about it. Let that be his private nightmare to carry. He felt startled when he heard himself ask if Jumbo thought God hid at night in places like the gorge. Jumbo, sighing, replied that most days he wasn't even sure if God existed.

JOHN MICHAEL FLYNN also writes and publishes as Basil Rosa. His book of essays, *How The Quiet Breathes*, was published in 2020 by New Meridian Arts. In 2017, he was Writer in Residence at Carl Sandburg's home, Connemara, in North Carolina. He's published poetry collections, and three short story collections, including *Dreaming Rodin*, and *Off To The Next Wherever*. His fourth collection, *Vintage Vinyl Playlist*, is forthcoming from Fomite (www.fomitepress.com).

The Old Timers
Rebecca Holcomb

In their retirement, the old timers maintained a permanent residence along Shug Bayou, and they didn't understand why Mr. Ned was going off to Vietnam.

"He made a family there while in the war," Yeller said once.

"He went broke taking care of Jan, needs somewhere cheap to die," others guessed, always when Mr. Ned wasn't around.

Shug Bayou's entrance is hidden off the main road in town, so discrete that if you weren't from this part of Louisiana, you'd have trouble finding it. A right at Tobacco Plus off the main road leads you down a long-twisted one lined with residential homes. Way down this road on the left is a small concrete bridge cutting into a dense wall of forest, a forest so deep and green that it could be mistaken for the back line of trees on someone's unmanaged property because of the "No Trespassing" sign posted near the entrance. But if you are from here, and you have a reason, then go on ahead.

Soon the busy world turns to hunting and fishing camps, outposts lining a slow-moving slug of a river, its surface adorned with lily pads and violently green moss, with thick reeds congregating well into the middle of it, and oaks, overburdened with spanish moss, seeming like solemn old men with beards watching from the banks, and cypress knees budging up to the surface to breathe like muddy stalactites. Some camps are dilapidated trailers with metal roofs built over their frames, and others are nicer, built up on beams with adjoining wooden docks. Most yards have a few rust buckets or tractors, perhaps a burn bin or an outdoor kitchen of sorts. Out there on Shug, it is common for a hound to run up to you off leash, for an old man speaking Cajun French to hand you moonshine.

Despite the trashiness of Shug Bayou, it is a place for weekend living, where things only get stolen if the guy had it coming, and trouble leaves you alone unless you go looking for it. But the group of men at Jimmy's camp, near the entrance of Shug, was a good bunch. They were looking for one last hoorah before Mr. Ned was boarding the plane next week. Even Jimmy's daddy, Mr. Rich Man Frank, was there to hunt and fish, though he had a nicer camp at the big lake, on the Texas side, where the bass have a chance of outswimming the alligators and gars.

They were sitting around in the front yard, drinking, cooking, and waiting for the afternoon to die down before they went fishing during an unusually warm fall. Mr. Ned and Jimmy discussed the possibility of hunting while the others fished.

It wasn't long before they had enough beers to return to why Mr. Ned was leaving, as though he had already gone, even though he stood in his usual rim rod way, looking like a real-life Clint Eastwood, by a gardenia bush Lily planted two years ago, the fragrance the little white flowers put off being her, "All-time favorite." To Jimmy's bewilderment, his wife's lasting obsession with the plant led to her suggesting they name their first child, due any day now, Gardenia.

"He's only going to 'Nam to get outta helpin' with that new dock down at the boat
launch," Yeller said. His belly lurched as he struggled to get up from his lawn chair to stir the cracklins' frying over the fire, the grease bubbling as he added additional contributions of pork to the vat.

"Shit," Mr. Ned paused, watching the bubbles. "Y'all fat asses might need to do a bit of exercising, consider it a blessing."

"You hear that, boys?"

Yeller turned to the other men with excitement, "Old Ned thinks we're fat!"

They laughed.

They had hurt feelings at Mr. Ned's refusal to tell why he was leaving the best country in the world, and why he was leaving them. But Mr. Ned didn't have the words to tell his reasons.

So, instead he was drinking heavy, maybe on his tenth *Milwaukee's Best*.

"Don't let those men fool you. That's some big ol' babies out there," Lily said a time ago. She had to stay home this weekend, bedridden from the pregnancy. She promised she'd be fine, but Jimmy went to kiss her on the way out, and she turned her head away, eyes fixed on HGTV, her legs swollen and propped up on pillows. He didn't need much more than that to get gone.

Even with Mr. Ned leaving, and this being his last weekend with him, Jimmy did feel a tang of guilt, leaving her swollen like that. He hoped he could find a solution to their marital distress while hunting in the woods, a place beyond domestic trials. Or in the kind of knowledge only the old timers knew. Mostly, Jimmy wanted to trudge on like the rest, traditional, but Lily thought the word tradition was often applied like a flimsy band-aid over the deepest of wounds. Lily also believed in ghosts. Thought Louisiana was cursed from the past and full of ghosts. Lily would wring her hands hearing crying coyotes because she thought of them as harbingers of evil. Believed too, that modern day poverty, illness, stupidity, and violence was a curse from bad doings in the past: from Slavery to the Civil War and on. Lily said the South had some deep healing to do. She had a way of complicating everything, stressing herself silly over the simplest things.

So today, Jimmy was drinking heavy, too.

Suddenly Hank, the most hickish of them, pulled up in his rusted truck. He stepped out, his trucker hat reading *Beers and Deers,* and his overalls sagging over his withering frame, beer in hand. He greeted the men by raising his aged arm holding a beer in their direction. They all hooted and lifted their beers up in unison.

"And this one is for you, Mr. Ned!" Hank pointed at Mr. Ned and chugged the rest of his beer, wiping his thin lips with the back of his long, thin hand before running the hand through his long white beard. Mr. Ned laughed. His white hair was neatly combed under his hat lining the collar of a denim Wrangler button-up, long-sleeved shirt; even in the heat, he always wore long-sleeved shirts. Small in stature, he carried himself like a little hawk, his eyes moving steadily in their sockets, always observing, as though he was up higher than the rest, but even so, the men had respect for him. He received the Purple Heart from the war. He took care of Jana well into the stages of her dementia. Collected her home when she strayed into neighbors' yards in her nightgown. Never complained. Rarely spoke about himself.

He had lived most of his life on Shug Bayou, dug out the ditches and cleared roads after storms with his tractor for the community. If you were lucky, he'd make you his famous breakfast sandwich with the tomatoes grown from his garden when he took you fishing. But the lines on his face were jagged and hard, a constant shadow pervaded under his eyes. Yet, some of the others seemed to be caricatures in comparison, lacked the integrity that Mr. Ned seemed to naturally have, and he knew the best spots for catfishing. Jimmy's dad was never there, too good for them. Yeller was a fat hick. Jones was lonesome as hell, and it was just sad. Cray was short for Crazy, did some time in prison, no teeth, most likely had a mental illness. Most were functioning alcoholics. But none of that mattered because they all had, at some point in time, given away part of themselves without asking for much in return.

Paper plates were plopped down on the card table Jimmy had put out. The men sat in a circle, eating in the shade.

When Hank got situated in his chair, he pulled out a flask filled with Old Charter and handed it around. He lit a cigarette while the others chewed. They waited for him to start up. It was the one thing that plagued him: not his meth head sister, not his lack of money, not the constant grind his life had been reduced to. Nor was it his permanent shack in the woods that had no running water.

But, oh, *Bev-er-ly*. She was so important that every syllable of her name required profound emphasis.

"You know *Bev-er-ly* is raising her sister's kids now?" he said.

"Why the hell she doin' that?" Yeller asked. The flesh on his massive double chin trembled as he gulped down his food.

"Drugs, yessir. Her sister is riddled with 'em,'" he said. "A good goddamn woman that Bev-er-ly."

The men nodded. They all knew someone bad off.

"You know she had standards and expectations and whatnot for me, like to stop the drinking." He took another long sip of beer and winked towards the ground at his ineptitude, as though it was embodied in his shadow.

"Women are the Devil!" Jones blurted out; his lonesome mouth situated in a permanent pout. Yeller slapped his hollow chest to shut up.

Jimmy thought about this generalization. He always considered women to be like the yellow wildflowers growing off 49 in the tall grass, not the wrecks that frequent the interstate. At least Lily was this way to him, despite their differences.

"Not all women," Hank said. He did his knee slapping thing, the thing he always did as soon as he brought her up, embarrassed. They knew he was leaving when he got up and threw away his plate.

"I kid you not," he said as he walked to his truck like Johnny Cash walking off the stage before an encore, drunk, going down the dirt road to sleep it off in his shack. He opened the door, got in, and shut it. Then he did it again, as though he forgot, or maybe for good measure. They could see him fumbling inside the cab to roll the window down manually. He finally started up the engine. Over the dull roar he hollered out the window, almost hitting a tree, "I kid you not. I'll get her back!"

"Sure, you will Hank," the old timers murmured like they were all saying "amen" in church. It was unclear if Hank heard them, if he found their somber reply as odd as his torment. You'd think someone would poke fun at Hank, but they all out of friendliness, or from broken hearts themselves, prayed that she would take him back.

The old timers began moseying about, preparing to go fishing. Jimmy helped them load the boat with gear but decided to stay behind. He laughed as they hauled their rickety bodies up the ladder, some cursing more than others, and into the pontoon boat his daddy had brought.

Daddy had money and respect in the parish. He was a petroleum engineer who travelled for most of Jimmy's childhood, saving the family farm by being able to fund its operations without banks. He was always working in strange countries, so Jimmy had to pick up the slack on the farm while he was away. If he didn't, he'd pay when daddy returned. Mamma was in a quilting club with Mr. Ned's wife and some other ladies whose husbands spent their weekends on Shug. While she worked with the ladies, Mr. Ned would take Jimmy hunting or fishing, usually him and Tom Laborde, Ms. Susie's son, his best friend.

Everyone was gone. Jimmy was sitting alone in a lawn chair, wondering in a drunken haze where Mr. Ned was. They were supposed to go hunting together. Had Mr. Ned gone fishing instead? He looked about the camp. The fire was out but still smoking. Shadows grew into the color of dark bruises with the approaching darkness. The wind whooshed the leaves about the yard, and the swing down at the dock where he first kissed Lily swayed, like a ghost sat on it, swinging its heels.

Guilt rattled Jimmy's chest thinking of Lily alone at home. He thought of the hell he put her through lately, the constant irritation he felt as she prepared for the baby, the nagging feeling of not being ready. Trying to sort it out, he'd drive in contemplation across the Atchafalaya bridge towards his folks' land. Passing fields of sugar cane, their stalks like church spires pointing up towards a mean god.

He would get to their house and his daddy waved slowly from his rocking chair on the porch as he drove to the back field. Mama might be watching from the kitchen window as she fixed supper. Jimmy knew he should suffer silently, not let them see and worry. But watching the sun set over the pasture behind the house where he grew up made him feel better--though he would never be able to afford the hay to feed the hundreds of cows that graze there. There he would sit in the driver's seat of his truck with a beer and think unhappy things: about his best friend, Tom, who died from an opioid overdose that last July, or the time his father beat him when he came home and heard Jimmy lost a calf and mother during a birth gone wrong--ashamed and angry because Jimmy was unable to remedy the simple breech without him--until darkness reminded him of work the next morning.

Jimmy realized that he had been sulking in the lawn chair for too long, waiting for Mr. Ned to appear from the trailer. But Mr. Ned must have went fishing instead. Jimmy must not have seen.

He staggered to his truck and pulled out of the front drive. He was swerving down the dirt road that led out of the camp, and he no longer felt certain about anything. He swallowed hard at what was to come, thought about how even good intentioned parents, like his own daddy, fail. He pulled the truck over and grabbed his hunting gear out of the bed, and then he walked into the woods.

The sun had set an hour ago, it was illegal to hunt now, but the crunch of leaves underfoot made what he was doing feel natural. Maybe he needed to gather the remaining hints of child within him and say goodbye and so long. As he walked, he envisioned all the parts of himself, even the microscopic atom and molecule, moving together in ways that made me him feel superhuman. In the woods, he is free. He can feel the air trace the back of his exposed neck. He can hear the smallest animal, an ant, bulldozing a path through the forest floor. In the woods, a squirrel barking to his companion seems like a real language. The squawks from two blackbirds circling and dashing the petioles of a palmetto bush, a dramatic symphony.

An evil spirit had possession of Jimmy that night, or that year, or maybe just that season. There were too many missed opportunities: a buck would caress a highlighted section of forest, and then disappear behind a hickory. Or a doe would saunter on the edge of a shallow ravine only to fall back the moment the scope was on her. In one moment, he would be watching a red cardinal hop about in a daze, and then in another, was wiping a tear pulling at his left eye at a tangle of vines suffocating a grove of old oaks. For every beautiful thing in the world there was twice as much evil. How was he going to protect his—hell, they couldn't even agree on a name—from it?

But there was only darkness. Darkness and all those spirits Lily talks about. A coyote cried, and there was movement up ahead. He slinked his body toward it. Hunting in the dark is not fair for the deer. He knew it. The old timers knew it. Everyone knew. But the spirits had him. Jimmy situated himself to take aim at the deer's shadow, felt his hand lifting his thirty-thirty. He took a breath like he was told to do his entire life before shooting, but suddenly, the shadow changed. Well, it stood, and what Jimmy saw was not a deer, but a Confederate soldier, his long gun pointed directly at Jimmy--a ghost illuminated in an otherworldly glow, his blue gray torso stained with blood from a hole in his nine-buttoned jacket. Another hole was in the soldier's cap, next to his bomb badge shining brighter than the ghost's other apparel. Jimmy lowered his gun and gulped. The ghost let out a rip-roaring laugh, like a madman. So unsettling was the laugh, and so loud, that the birds flew from their nests and the trees seemed to buckle. The ghost walked towards Jimmy, but the leaves didn't crunch when he stepped. The world was muted, the wind gone out, the moonlight seemed to only be emanating from the ghost.

"You dead or alive son?" The ghost asked.

Jimmy didn't respond.

"Dead?" the ghost questioned. "Or Alive?"

"Alive."

"You a liar?"

"No sir."

"You seem mighty dead to me, let's see if my assumption is correct."

And with that, the Ghost shot Jimmy and he fell to the ground.

"SON," A VOICE SAID. He heard that voice before, it was there when he pulled a 15-pound catfish in, when he was a kid skinning a squirrel for the first time. It was always there.

"Son… Jimmy, why you down on the ground," Mr. Ned said shaking him. "Jesus, you hurt?"

"I'm fine, just passed out," Jimmy said and stood. "Had too much to drink, I'm ok."

"You sure?" Mr. Ned asked. "We thought you might be in trouble since it's so late. Everyone is looking for you."

"Nothing is wrong, I must have just passed out." Jimmy was wondering if Mr. Ned saw the ghost too.

"What's wrong?" Mr. Ned asked. "Never mind, let's get on to truck before the Warden comes."

On the walk back, Jimmy was trying to rehearse the words to tell Mr. Ned what happened. It was too absurd to talk about, so maybe he ought to lie. But when they got to the cab of the truck, there was nothing Jimmy could do but tell Mr. Ned about the ghost and the fear of the birth, about his inadequacy and his curses. Mr. Ned didn't rush Jimmy off to the actual birth that was happening at that moment, the real reason the men were searching for Jimmy, as Lily had called from the hospital saying she went into labor. Mr. Ned listened and nodded in that old timer way to the troubles that were driving Jimmy half mad. A list too long to mention. A list that touches us all one time or another.

"What are you going to Vietnam for?" Jimmy asked.

"To get rid of them demons. Words can't do it right. Rest assured poaching a deer, or seeing a ghost, is not as scary," Mr. Ned looked out the window, into the darkness, "as killing a person is. What I did." Mr. Ned shook his head. "I don't want to be ashamed when I die. Gotta fix things for some families I hurt over there."

"You can't go to church and fix it that way?" Jimmy said.

"I already tried, son. God ain't lazy and neither am I."

They sat there in the silence for a few moments.

"Your Daddy was always a SOB, living in his head," Mr. Ned said. "Too distant to be a real father, like his heart wasn't in it."

"I know it," Jimmy said.

"Choose to be present, for all of it," he said, putting the truck in drive. "Now, time to get you to the hospital, away from these ghosts."

The pair drove out of Shug, took the long way, avoiding the main drag. Fields of sugar cane and cotton illuminated in moonlight blurred by. Jimmy rolled down his window, and the cool night air calmed him. He thought about Mr. Ned leaving and the ghost in the forest--if it was real or if he crazy. What if Mr. Ned dies over there? Jimmy knew he and this land were tied together until the day he is put in it. But Mr. Ned didn't seem worried about what comes next, or where he will be laid to rest. He seemed certain in the decisions he made. Maybe it was more important to think on the living.

A FEW SLEEPLESS WEEKS LATER, Lily and Jimmy decided to go to the camp for the first time with baby Gardenia. Hank pulled up into the driveway with Be-ver-ly in his passenger seat. Jimmy didn't know what he was expecting, but the beautiful black woman with a length of intricate braids falling down her back was not it. She was wearing a pair of overalls with a flannel shirt underneath the bib, and it looked like Hank had washed his jacket. Jimmy greeted Be-ver-ly with, "I've heard a lot about you," and she met him with a knowing chuckle.

Jimmy stood there watching while they unloaded the poles and some shiners. He followed them down to the dock and they pulled up some chairs. What surprised him the most about the couple was how silent they were, as though they went through hell and came out on the other side of it. Hank reached in the Styrofoam ice chest not for a beer, but for a shiner to bait her hook. He cracked a few jokes, and her laugh was hearty and musical, like a drum beating.

Jimmy began to feel hopeful. He wished Mr. Ned could see he got her back, but Mr. Ned had already left this part of the world for another. A sense of relief flooded through Jimmy, thinking of him rectifying his mistakes. Or maybe, just connecting with himself. An image of Mr. Ned floating in the ocean, the salt easing into his joints, and a pleasant breeze bouncing off his forehead made Jimmy smile.

He looked at the pair out of the corner of his eye in between casts, having joined in on the fishing for a few minutes while the baby slept, a baby monitor attached to his hip, ready for Gardenia's awakening cry. Lily watched from her hammock, taking a moment to relax. He didn't tell her about the ghost, though he was sure it happened. Hank caught Jimmy studying them and winks, reminded of his previous drunkenness in this mannerism and considers how tomorrow it may all go back to shit. But for now, Jimmy chose to see it the way the old timers would: as a transformation, a renewal, a gift.

Rebecca Holcomb is currently pursuing her MFA at Florida State University where she is nonfiction co-editor at *The Southeast Review*. Previously, she taught high school throughout Louisiana and obtained an MAT from Northwestern State University.

Speck, WV
Timothy Dodd

> *For now we see in a mirror dimly, but then face to face.*
> *Now I know in part; then I shall know fully, even as I*
> *have been fully known.*
>
> —*1 Corinthians 13:12*

In the little town founded along the Greenbrier River thirty years before the Civil War, Barren and Fern Funeral Home stood as its stateliest building. No courthouse or old bank building bested its lovely, baby blue, Second Empire grace. Raywin entered the funeral parlor with no interest in its beauty, however, taking a flyer from the marble counter in the vestibule. Flowery lettering across the top of the paper read: "In Loving Memory of Calhoun Ruff."

Raywin walked into the large reception room and sat down in one of the few remaining seats in the back. The brass-handled, black casket lay open up front, surrounded by a lush array of flowers. Beside Raywin sat an elderly man in a brown suit draped over his gaunt body, long fingernails crawling out from the sleeves.

"A shame what happened to Cal, ain't it?" the man said, his hands resting on his thighs, fingers moving as if he played the harp.

"Sure is. Dying is hard for everyone," Raywin replied.

"Ain't nobody deserves to go out that way. Good man though."

"I bet."

"What do you mean you bet? Didn't you know him?"

"No, I never met him," Raywin answered, turning back toward the casket.

"Oh, you're just a friend of a friend or something?"

An organ sounded and Raywin took a deep breath, wiping his brow with the back of his hand. Two clergymen stood up and positioned themselves near the podium, but a minute later the organist stopped, the ministers returned to their seats, and the old man beside Raywin continued.

"Who you with here anyway, if you don't mind me asking?"

"By myself."

"So, what's your connection to Cal then?"

"Don't have much."

The old man lowered his voice to a whisper. "So, what are you doing here, son? Why ain't you out shooting pool, driving around, or hunting for a lady?"

"I'm a seeker of life," Raywin replied.

The man paused and gave Raywin the lookover. "Young man, you know this is a funeral?"

"Can't know much about life without knowing something about death."

"Well, I guess that's true, but I never heard of somebody going to a funeral without knowing the deceased. Truth told, I'm not sure they'd want you here."

The ministers stood and music started for a second time. Introductions and "How Great Thou Art" followed. Reverend Sank Caldron then gave a eulogy, but clichés about the dead man's character riled Raywin—he'd heard them at the last funeral: "He'd give you the shirt off his back" and "You don't find people like him anymore."

When Reverend Cauldron finished, Raywin joined a line to view the deceased, taking deeper breaths as he got closer to the coffin. When he peered over into the casket, Calhoun Ruff's face appeared tense, and his hands looked like he wore translucent gloves to mask wounds or decay. Raywin stared, saying nothing, then returned to his seat as visitors sang "To God Be the Glory."

A tug on his arm came as the song finished. Raywin turned, expecting to see the old man again, but instead a young blonde woman stared at him with a scowl.

"Somebody said you didn't know my daddy. You're just here stirring up trouble," she said, her voice scratchy. Raywin didn't respond. "Well? What's it about? Why are you here?"

"Just contemplating. Contemplating life. I'm a seeker."

"And you think my daddy's funeral is the place for that?" Behind the young woman, two men wheeled the casket out the back door of the funeral home.

"Well, I don't mean to offend anyone, but I'm trying to understand life better, and I figure that means I should know something about dying as well."

"Yeah, well you don't have to do it around here. Find someone else's funeral. Heck, find a cave or a field of wildflowers for all I care—they've got dead things in them, too. Hey, Charlie! Come here a second. This guy...what's your name?"

"Raywin."

A well-built man in a navy, three-piece suit strolled over.

"Raywin what?"

"Raywin Beet."

"This Mr. Beet don't even know Daddy. Just decided to show up."

"This is a funeral, fellow," the man said. A mole danced on his cheek when he spoke. "The family is in mourning, so if you didn't know our daddy, move on. You're not wanted here."

Raywin didn't answer and walked back through the vestibule, the first time his funeral visits had ended in confrontation. Exiting through the grand double doors of the funeral home, he lifted his hand to shield his eyes from the sun. The clouds had rolled back and the morning heated up.

A BURGUNDY EL CAMINO PULLED UP near Raywin, tires screeching and its back seat cluttered with boxes and junk. A thin-faced man with a long arm reached across the passenger's seat to roll down the window. Raywin didn't recognize the man or the car.

"What do you say, young fellow? You aren't deep in thought, are you?" the man asked, his voice high-pitched and his teeth looking as though he'd eaten raspberries.

Raywin shook his head, staring at the man's moss green suit and black fedora pulled over his brow.

"I'd like to have a word with you. Mind getting in the car?"

"I'd prefer not to," Raywin answered.

"Won't take long, my friend. Just a gentle conversation for a moment or two."

"No, I'm in the middle of a walk."

"Oh yeah? Out here ruminating on eternity, are you? Where you walking? Convenience store?"

"Actually I am. And not going anywhere in particular. I just like walking."

"Oh, okay. I figured you needed some coffee or a Snickers. Thought I could park this mad machine and we'd join forces."

The man turned off his engine and got out of the car. Thin as a month-old cadaver and maybe the tallest person Raywin had ever seen, he looked neither young nor old. His black Balmorals clicked on the crack-filled sidewalk as he stepped near the storefront of Hunt's Vacuum Cleaners, nauseating Raywin with his strong cologne. Two warts blocked half of a small tattoo on his left hand—Raywin thought it might be the skeleton of a fish.

"Might be your lucky day," the man said, following after Raywin who had resumed walking at a moderate pace. Empty streets and the mid-afternoon quiet had put the shops around them to sleep.

"Listen, I'm not the person to try any hard sells on."

"No, no, of course not," the man replied, hands in his pockets jingling coins. "But you're no fool either, and I'm sure you know life can go up or down with little more than the snap of a finger." Raywin imagined the man pulling a pogo stick out from under his hat. "In any case, I know you're a young guy who thinks about his purpose in life."

"Yes, that's true," Raywin confirmed, somewhat impressed.

"Very noble of you. And would you happen to have a social security card?"

"Not on me, no."

"No, no, of course not. I mean tucked away at home in some old, faded dresser under piles of flannel shirts and tube socks that aren't so white anymore."

"That's about right," Raywin replied. "Had it since I was twelve when my mother took me down to the bank one Saturday afternoon."

"Good, good. Is your mother an Ernest Tubbs fan by any chance?"

"Not particularly, no."

"How about you? You a singer?"

"Not really."

"Well that's not so important anyway. You got any skills with your hands?"

"What do you mean?" Raywin stopped and leaned against a parking meter. Nearby, A Bunch of Grapes Cafe had their chalkboard stand on the sidewalk with specials of the day advertised. "And what's the point of all this? You didn't even tell me your name or where you come from."

"Just stick with me a little longer and it will all make sense, son. And if you've got any ability with woodworking, fixing cars, appliances, anything like that, you'd better tell me."

"I've got some experience in bricklaying. That's about it. I'm all right with bicycles too. I'm not really interested in all that though."

"All right. That's good. Those are skills. That might actually do," the man said, pulling back his sleeves to check his watch, revealing another fish skeleton.

"Do what?" Raywin asked.

"You see, young buck, out past Skoal Run I'm building me an estate up on the ridge. That means there's a lot of work to be done, but it isn't easy finding the kind of quality help I need. Hard to find good people these days. You can hardly trust folks."

"I'm not interested in any of that," Raywin said, raising his voice.

"Well now don't dismiss things so fast. I have another gentleman doing most of the work. He's doing the bricklaying too, in fact. You'd just be a helper to him and all. Easy work. And I'll pay you twenty bucks an hour. Plus lunch is on me up at the house any day you're working there. Not to mention you'd learn a lot of skills from this other guy that you could use later on. Calhoun Ruff's his name."

"Calhoun Ruff?"

"Yep."

Raywin stopped and turned to face the man. "Calhoun Ruff's dead."

"What do you mean he's dead? He's working on my estate as we speak."

"No, no. I was at his funeral yesterday morning."

"Funeral? I just saw him on Friday. Look here, I even got his business card in my wallet." From a skinny, black wallet with a dancing skeleton on its exterior, the man took out a professionally designed business card, white with red letters, and handed it to Raywin.

Raywin read, "Calhoun Ruff: Fix-it Man," as he recalled the closed eyes and face of the corpse. "Middle-aged? Graying, thinning hair parted on the side?" he asked.

"Yep, that's him."

"He's purely dead. I saw him yesterday in his casket."

The man lifted his fedora to scratch a bald head with a noticeable number of stitches above the right ear, then ran back to his car, his lower jaw quivering. "You best watch yourself now, son," he called out, lowering his lanky body into the front seat. Raywin stood and watched in dismay as the man turned on the ignition and sped away.

Officer Cowden's police car floated into the parking lot, stopping near the gate to the city park. He got out of his vehicle on a mission, straightening his shirt and pulling his pants up by the belt. Raywin sat on a bench surrounded by tall maples and elms near the park's waterless fountain. Journal open on his lap, he fidgeted as Cowden approached.

"Mr. Beet?" the policeman sneered, his young face sunburned.

"Yes? Afternoon, Officer Cowden."

Cowden parked his strut directly in front of Raywin, his belt buckle about two feet from the youth's nose. "Tell me, how did you come to know a fellow by the name of Calhoun Ruff?"

"I didn't." Raywin looked down at the park bench where a line of ants flowed, hard at work. "I mean, I don't really know him."

"What do you mean you don't know him? You were at his funeral."

"I didn't go there because of knowing him."

"So now why the hell else would you go to a man's funeral if you didn't know him?" Cowden asked, arms folded and sweat stains streaked down the side of his shirt.

"I go to funerals because I'm trying to figure out some things," Raywin said. Behind him, an acorn hit the ground.

"Figure out some things like what?"

"Like things about life and death."

"And you're telling me that's why you went to Calhoun Ruff's funeral? And that otherwise you don't know the man?" Officer Cowden shifted his weight to his left foot and looked out across the park grounds.

"Yes, that's right."

"I tell you, this town gets crazier every day. Walnut Festival in September, two Mexican grocery stores. Now you. Do you go to every stranger's funeral in town?" Officer Cowden flicked his head towards an elderly woman in a long, floral night dress who had stopped to let her mutt urinate. "You going to go to her funeral too?"

"I guess I might if she passes away."

Officer Cowden bent over to look Raywin in the eye, his eyebrows reminding the young man of crabgrass. "You might," Officer Cowden said, poorly mimicking Raywin's voice.

"Yeah."

The little dog nearby yelped a couple of times and kicked up some grass. "Of course she's gonna pass away. I guess you *might* know a little something about Calhoun Ruff being murdered too."

"Murdered?" Raywin shook his head several times. "No, I had no idea he was murdered."

"So you're saying you didn't have anything to do with that?"

"If I didn't know about it, then I didn't have nothing to do with it, Officer."

"That's queer."

"What's queer?"

Cowden raised his voice. "Hey, are you getting smart with an officer of the law?"

"No, I'm just minding my business and you're making insinuations."

"We can make them down at the police station if you'd prefer. You ever been down there before?"

"Just driving by."

"Just driving by, huh?"

"Yeah."

"You know what? I ought to search you." Raywin bit his lower lip, remembering that Calhoun Ruff's card, along with a few nickels, rested in his front pocket. "You own a car?"

"No, never had one."

"Well that's good because I suggest you don't go very far in the next few weeks. We'll be wanting to have an official word with you. This here word is just unofficial."

Raywin sat expressionless, contemplating the difference.

"It's a-fixing to rain," Officer Cowden said, turning to walk back to his vehicle. "In the meantime, maybe you might want to start searching for some alerbi."

TWO WEEKS AFTER THE FUNERAL, Calhoun Ruff's daughter found

Raywin walking his usual route on Main Street, slowly stepping in the shadows of the town's decrepit, turn-of-the-century, two-story buildings. Raywin didn't recognize her. She hadn't looked particularly well-to-do in her black dress at the funeral, but now she looked downright haggard in places. Her halter top and flip-flops revealed a bulging stomach and several deformed toes with worn off, dark blue nail polish. There was a band-aid wrapped around the fourth toe of her left foot. She wore oversized sunglasses, and her hair was pulled back and tied in a tight bun.

"I knew I'd find you eventually," she said, grabbing Raywin by the arm in front of the dark, cobwebbed doorway of Billy's Shoe Store, closed for nearly a decade. "Remember me?"

"Of course."

"I just got paid last night, and you're coming with me to DQ."

"No, no. I'll have to pass. I've got some thinking to do. Plus I've only got some small change."

"Don't worry, it's on me. And we'll do your thinking together. I know I didn't treat you so nicely the other day."

"That's all right. You had your reasons. You sure you can afford an extra mouth at DQ?"

"Depends how much you eat," she said, tilting her head to the side with a smile.

Raywin giggled. "Not much really. We could just get a couple blueberry soda pops up there at McCrory's. Or I can just get a sundae at DQ and pay for half of it. Then you could eat the other half."

"Deal."

The girl walked much faster than Raywin as she immediately set off toward the Dairy Queen two blocks away. Raywin quickly fell behind, thinking how much shorter she was without heels. She whistled as he followed her, and the handful of people on the sidewalks—all but one a senior citizen with a walker, crutches, or wheelchair—stopped and stared as she passed.

"You got a cigarette?" she yelled back.

"I've got Husky."

The girl didn't answer and instead started sprinting when she passed B&S Bank. She ran the last block and turned the corner to the Dairy Queen entrance where two El Caminos and two Chevy Novas sat parked in the lot. When Raywin caught up he found her holding the door open for him, the newly planted morning glories at the entrance already trampled on.

"You're not in too much hurry to get that half-price sundae," she said.

"What's the rush? Dairy Queen's not going out of business."

"They aren't, but we are," she replied. "You remember we met at a funeral, right? Now grab us a booth." Raywin sat down in the first booth inside the doorway. "Jesus, can't you pick a place a little more private?" the girl asked, bypassing him for a spot in the rear corner of the store away from other customers.

Raywin got up and followed. When he sat down across from her, a large, laminated menu hid her face. "I hate it how their strawberry sauce always looks so bloody," she said.

"The blueberry sauce looks bloody too."

The girl lowered her oversized piece of plastic to peep at Raywin. "What?"

"Horseshoe crabs have blue blood."

"Hey, that reminds me. Are you planning to go to any more strangers' funerals? I might like to go with you to one." Raywin followed the girl's hands as she placed the menu back in the rack against the wall, then put them under the table.

A waitress wearing a lopsided apron loaded with ketchup stains came over and interrupted the conversation. Raywin thought her hair looked especially fine. "Can I get you all anything to drink to start off?" she asked.

"No, my man and me are just having some sundaes. What kind you want, Beet?"

"Banana."

"Banana?"

"I always get banana."

"All right. Make it one banana for Beet and a hot fudge for me. Medium-sized."

The waitress scribbled a few words on a tiny notepad with her oversized pen. "You all want nuts on them?"

"What kind of a question is that? Of course we do. I want lots of nuts and so does he. Right, Beet?"

"Sure."

"Okay, that'll be two medium sundaes with extra nuts. One banana and one hot fudge. Anything else? Sodas or something to drink?"

"No, you already asked us that," the girl answered, one hand now fiddling with the saltshaker. By the way her other arm moved under the table, Raywin knew she was scratching her leg.

"Okay, then. Be just a few minutes and I'll bring those little treats out for you all."

"You know, Beet, I really hate them advertising posters they stick up in these places," the girl said as the waitress walked away.

"Don't seem real, do they?" Raywin said. Several times since meeting the girl he had wondered if he should ask about her father and how the family was doing, about the news of murder, but she always got her questions out quicker than he did.

"No, they don't," she replied, leaning across the table to look at his face more closely. "Hey, you remember you told me you're a seeker of life, right?"

"Right."

"You think there's people out there then who are seekers of death, Beet?" Raywin didn't answer as a fluorescent light above the table flickered. "Well, do you? Why do you always have to take so long to answer a question or keep the conversation going? Don't you know it pays to be quick on your toes? Why do you think mine are all screwed up? I know you've seen them."

"I guess so."

"You guess what?"

"I guess there are seekers of death. I don't see why not. There are people out there who seek for anything."

"Well, wouldn't a seeker of death just find it and die? That'd be the end of it."

"Not necessarily."

"You think a seeker of life and a seeker of death could ever get along then?"

"Seems like it'd be kind of difficult maybe," Raywin replied. "I doubt one would be very interested in the other."

The girl leaned back from the table as if relieved to get an answer to a burning question. "You're no seeker of life then," she said.

Raywin kept his eyes down on the table. "Sure I am. What makes you say that?"

"Somebody killed my daddy, you know."

"That's what I heard."

"He wasn't no seeker of life. That's for sure. And I'm not either."

"I don't know. I never met him. The reverend sure painted him as a pretty righteous fellow."

"They all do that. Even the serial killers get bragged on at their funerals. Don't mean it's true." A teenage couple came in giggling and sat down two booths over from Raywin and the girl. "To tell you the truth, I'm not here to get into all that. I was just kind of curious."

"Curious about what?"

The waitress returned. Without speaking, she laid down two napkins, then two long-necked spoons, and finally the two sundaes with extra nuts, the hot fudge in front of Raywin.

Raywin looked across at the girl's turned up nose. "Go ahead and try the banana," he said.

"No, that's okay," the girl replied, switching the sundaes.

"Listen, Ms. Ruff…"

"Call me by my name. It's Candy."

"Listen, Candy. Just so you know, I went to a lot of funerals before your father's. I wasn't trying to pick on him or on you. It's just something I do."

"We already talked about all that. Let's just drop it and enjoy our sundaes, okay? I been working hard doing meaningless lawn care and helping build this new house outside of town. Laying low. I need to relax a little bit. There isn't nobody who doesn't have but a limited amount of time."

Raywin agreed and dipped into his sundae. Conversation died as Candy doubled him in bites, and when Raywin looked up again, the door to the men's restroom creaked open at the end of a hallway. He recognized the tall, lean man poking his bald head out before crossing in front of the cash registers, black shoes clicking on the tile. A mixed scent of Brut and human waste floated out with him, strong enough for a whiff to reach Raywin and Candy.

"Stinks in here half the time," Candy said with almost half of her sundae finished. A minor commotion had started behind the counter, followed by the sound of a police siren in the distance. The siren steadily grew louder, and within two minutes a police car pulled up in the parking lot. Officer Cowden jumped out of his patrol car and yanked open the door to the Dairy Queen.

"Cheeseburger, no pickles, Eunice," he yelled. "I'm in a rush."

Candy slouched down in the booth and tried to hide behind her sundae.

The waitress scurried over to the policeman's side. "Don't you have time to sit down, sweetheart?"

"No, I don't," Cowden answered emphatically. "And where's the girl?"

Candy had stopped eating, and Raywin put his hand into his front pocket, feeling Calhoun Ruff's card again. He couldn't hear the waitress answer Officer Cowden, but she nodded in their direction.

Officer Cowden turned and looked back at Raywin and Candy. A wide grin slowly spread across his face, and his index finger twitched close to his gun like the tail of a dog in love.

TIMOTHY DODD is from Mink Shoals, West Virginia. He is the author of short story collections *Fissures and Other Stories* (Bottom Dog Press), *Men in Midnight Bloom* (Cowboy Jamboree Press), and *Mortality Birds* (Southernmost Books, with Steve Lambert), as well as the poetry collection, *Modern Ancient* (High Window Press) and *Vital Decay* (forthcoming, Cajun Mutt Press). Tim's stories have appeared in *Yemassee*, *Broad River Review*, and *Anthology of Appalachian Writers*; his poetry in *Crab Creek Review*, *Roanoke Review*, *Crannog*, and elsewhere. Also a visual artist, he primarily exhibits his oil paintings in the Philippines. Sample artwork can be found on Instagram @timothybdoddartwork. His website is timothybdodd.wordpress.com.

All the Pretty Things
Mindy Friddle
Previously Appeared in *storySouth*, 2022

THE GRANDMOTHER BELIEVED IN JESUS AND IN FACTS.

On her bookshelf: the King James Bible, an atlas, an illustrated medical dictionary, a farmers' almanac. No romance novels. No mysteries, no books about art or photography, no poetry. Nothing whimsical. Nothing to entertain.

The grandmother's books instructed her on life and the afterlife. You could read Scripture to accept Jesus Christ as your Lord and Savior. You could look up how to treat a plantar wart, identify a black widow spider, check the fall's frost date. You could locate Guatemala in Central America, where your Baptist church sent missionaries, and Saigon where your son was sent to war.

When her grandchildren were born, the grandmother bought a set of World Book Encyclopedias: twenty books that smelled of glue, edged in gold, filled with shiny colorful photographs and maps, diagrams of machines.

In this way, the grandmother hoped to impart how to survive in a world that was often ugly and always sinful. Facts at your fingertips could save you from ignorance and humiliation. Christ could save you from yourself.

The encyclopedias fascinated the children. The cellophane inserts of a frog's body, overlaid with blood vessels, muscles, and bones. The articles on elephants, airplanes, and Iceland. And later, the unit on "Reproduction" with its clinical but titillating description of intercourse.

But the volumes were soon outdated. The map of Africa was wrong, and the section on space travel—ridiculous!

THE GRANDMOTHER WAS BORN IN 1920, the year women got the vote and men lost liquor. She grew up on a hardscrabble farm in the foothills of South Carolina.

She left her crowded farmhouse at sixteen, moved into a rooming house, and worked at a textile mill. She was tired of taking care of her sisters and brothers. She did not care for children. She wanted to earn her own money, sleep in her own bed, buy her dresses, not sew them.

After three years, she married a local boy who left farming for soldiering in the Second World War. The grandmother's husband, a tank mechanic, fought in the Battle of Normandy.

When her grandchildren asked about this, about the war, about the grandmother's childhood and the Great Depression, the grandmother didn't want to talk about it. The grandmother only talked about the funny, good things, not the hard, dark parts of her life, which the grandchildren heard about from cousins.

Funny: The grandmother played basketball as a girl and had a photograph of herself in her uniform—baggy pantaloons, puffy sleeves.

Sad secret: The grandmother had loved playing basketball in school, the fierce competition, the brusque women's coach barking orders, even the miserable, modest uniforms. But she had to quit the team because sports and girls? Don't be silly.

Good: The grandmother recalled how her family's plow horse adored her father. How that horse nuzzled her father's arm and obeyed him, only him, no one else, not even her brother.

Shameful: The plow horse kept the grandmother's family alive, laboring with the grandmother's father, dawn until dusk, until both were covered in sweat and dirt. A bad harvest meant a bad year, it meant hunger and sickness. It meant crying babies, it meant death.

Good: The grandmother was an observant, church-going Baptist. She didn't drink alcohol, and believed no one else should, either. For any reason. No champagne toasts. No rum cakes. Also, no dancing. Even square dancing. Nope. And no gambling. No casinos, no friendly hands of poker, no lottery, no Bingo. Drinking ruined men, and therefore ruined families. Ditto for gambling. As for dancing, read Mark 6:17-28. Dancing is how John the Baptist's head ended up on a platter.

THE GRANDMOTHER TOOK PLEASURE IN DISPLEASURE. She believed happiness and hardship were yoked. You did not get one without the other.

She did not enjoy work, but it pleased her to endure it. A paycheck from forty hours of hell—a fair exchange. And the grandmother always worked—in the mill, as a telephone operator, as a secretary—jobs she found tedious and dreary, jobs she despised. In return: two acres, a new Plymouth, purchased with saved paychecks, from money not borrowed but earned, the only kind of money she trusted.

The grandmother did not fear poverty; she feared the shame of it. Like her father's plow horse, she labored tirelessly, blinkered and resolute. If you worked hard, followed man's rules and God's laws, you would prosper. Look around. Only criminals, drunken lay-abouts, unrepentant sinners, and the lazy were poor. The Lord rewarded your faith, your hard work and thrift. Owning your house and car—well, your neighbors could see for themselves you were a fine Christian.

Still, the grandmother struggled mightily with temptation. She prayed hard before she went shopping. She begged the Lord for self-control because she wanted to buy, buy, buy. This was after the war, boom times—everyone in high cotton. Every two weeks, on payday, the grandmother allowed herself to walk through the magnificent, marble-floored department stores downtown, appalled at her own lust for silk stockings, patent-leather pumps, pearl chokers, Revlon lipstick. As the grandmother stepped onto the stuttering, thrilling escalator of Meyers-Arnold, she felt as if a child inside her awakened, taking in the racks of dazzling dresses, the array of darling hats, the candy-colored Fiestaware, the flamingo pink polka-dotted swimsuit, the stoppered perfume bottles from Paris. *Look at all the pretties*, the child's voice inside her said. *I've been so good. Can I have that, and that, and that? I deserve it!* The grandmother recognized that voice of sin, tempting her to give in to fathomless desire, daring her to spend, to splurge. The spoiled, terrible child inside her needed thrashing and to be sent to bed without supper.

The grandmother reeled in her own ravenous buying impulses, kept an iron grip on her pocketbook, held sacred her budget, as any deviance could destroy her life, would bring the whole thing down. On each shopping trip, she allowed herself one carefully planned purchase: a pair of white gloves, a tie for her husband to wear to church, a Sunbeam toaster. And while she left the department store frustrated, yearning for more, more, more, the grandmother congratulated herself for resisting sin, for finding the strength to deny herself all the beautiful things, for muting that wicked child's voice.

Of course, the grandmother's enormous reservoir of self-discipline came at a price. It cost her curiosity. Impoverished her imagination. Drained her empathy. She resented those who let the greedy tyrant of a child inside them run amok and take over, people who grew fat, drunk, in debt. If she could overcome temptation, why couldn't they? Her introspection atrophied, her judgment calcified. Also, the grandmother cultivated a habit of denying beauty. She did not allow herself the luxury of visiting museums, listening to opera, learning the Foxtrot, watching movies, or reading about strange, dangerous ideas in the newspaper. She turned away from art in all its guises, for such beauty moved and disturbed her.

But as the years passed, the grandmother learned to curate beauty, of a sort. She sought elegance that pleased her, that she could collect, cherish, display. And like a curator, she kept her valuables behind glass, in locked cabinets, dusted and polished, to be admired and coveted, seldom used. For decades she scrimped, buying her objects d'art with cash, never credit. First, sterling silverware, fine china, a crystal pitcher imported from Ireland. Next, white carpet in the living room, porcelain vases, exquisite lamps. In her closet, fashionable dresses hung, splendid suits in sherbet pastels, matching hats and shoes, and in her vanity, Maybelline powders and creams, clip-on ear bobs, daisy brooches.

The grandmother cherished her resplendent wardrobe, yet dressed up only a few hours each week, for church. She reserved her fine china settings for Thanksgiving, Christmas, and Easter. The other 362 days of the year, her family ate on chipped plates. Plastic runners and accordion doors kept the white living room unsullied, pristine as snow. In this way, the grandmother cordoned off her life, preserving all the beautiful things, protecting them.

THE GRANDMOTHER WAS NOT HAPPY but, in the wake of an achievement or a purchase borne of her industriousness, occasionally appeared pleased.

Only when the grandmother prepared lunches for the grandfather did a rare look of tenderness cross her face. The grandchildren liked to watch this. First, the grandmother tucked the tough heel of leftover roast beef between soft white bread, slathered with Duke's mayonnaise. Next, the careful folding and pleating of wax paper around the sandwich, as if the grandmother were wrapping a gift. The grandmother poured iced tea into a thermos, then packed the grandfather's metal lunchbox, adding a watermelon rind pickle and something sweet, a square of homemade fudge, a slice of pound cake.

But mostly, there was no tenderness. There was no time for it. Weekdays, after work, and on Saturdays, the grandmother and the grandfather labored together in their garden, where there was always something urgent to plant, pick, put up, freeze, or can—bushels of okra, field peas, peppers, figs, cucumbers, tomatoes, squash, turnips, sweet potatoes. Gardening was not a hobby. There were no hobbies. There were chores. Even the grandfather's fishing was not leisurely but purposeful. Fish to cook, to store. The mess of bream and bass, the occasional catfish, cleaned and deboned, dipped in cornmeal, fried. The rest frozen, blocks of gleaming fish stacked, like fine, veined marble, in the spare freezer.

The grandmother kept this deep freezer in the garage, filled it with food grown or caught, her need to stockpile compulsive, urgent, inherited. She clipped coupons. She saved and saved and saved. The grandmother's parsimony was legendary.

That's why what happened later was so hard to believe.

THE GRANDMOTHER TURNED NINETY, a widow for twenty years. The radius of her life shrank into a hard dot, a pinpoint of lead. The obituary pages filled with familiar names, people she had liked or detested. Some weeks, she went to the mortuary more often than Winn-Dixie. The Baptist church's membership withered; the preacher went part-time. Young families moved into her neighborhood—from Mexico, Vietnam, India. Strange, spicy scents drifted into her yard at dinnertime. She heard foreign tongues bickering, proclaiming, celebrating.

The grandmother still drove her beige Chevrolet. She went to church, cooked for herself and for her grandchildren on Sundays. Twice a week, she carpooled with three friends, driving to the Y for senior aerobics. But the grandmother's carpool did not spill over into lunches or brunches or outings. The grandmother didn't cultivate female friends. She preferred the company of men.

Yet the men in her life kept disappearing. Her husband, lost to Alzheimer's. Her son retiring, moving away. Her brother dying peacefully of pneumonia at ninety, but still—how she had worshiped him, her older brother who slopped pigs with her, milked cows, taught her how to drive a tractor, who loved her fig preserves, who opened his own barber shop, thanks to the GI Bill, who raised four God-fearing children.

Next door to the grandmother, in a rental house, her nephew lived on disability, doing odd jobs for her, and gardening, the two of them working side by side for hours, every day, for a dozen years. One day, the nephew died of a heart attack. The grandmother was devastated. She took to her bed, and someone saw her cry.

The grandmother was alone, but she did not admit she was lonely. The grandmother believed loneliness was a sign of weakness. If you could not find comfort in prayer, your faith was failing. Jesus talked to you; it was your fault if you weren't listening.

In truth, the grandmother longed for the company of a man. A man content to follow her list of chores, her plans for the day; a man happy to labor by her side, hour by hour, as her brother had, her husband, her nephew.

THE GRANDMOTHER'S FAMILY BEGAN TO TALK to her about moving. About *options*. They worried about her living alone. She may not have enough money for nursing care if she chose to *age in place*. When she heard the words *retirement community* the grandmother became so enraged, she trembled. She would never leave her two acres, her ranch house, three apple trees, the collapsing shed, the patio she scrubbed with bleach every Saturday, never! She refused to sign a living will or a medical directive, and for months, she did not sign a power of attorney, as her son begged her to do. The grandmother went to her bookshelf to look up *aging in place* but could not find it.

So, she did what she'd always done when life was bleak and hard, she raked and dug holes and planted seeds, sowed, and reaped. Only, there was no husband at her side, no nephew. And the grandmother did not tolerate her family's hired helpers, men who stepped on her geraniums, parked on the grass.

Into this solitary toiling, this stubborn deflection of assistance, into this void, stepped the Grifter.

IN HER FRONT YARD, the grandmother raked leaves, wearing her dead husband's flannel shirt, her floppy hat, her tongueless Keds.

He struck up a conversation. Real nice place, he said. You keep this up all by yourself?

He offered to help her with yard work. For a few bucks.

That's how it started.

One hundred and twenty pounds, white male, mid-forties, five foot five. The first time the granddaughter saw him, at the arraignment hearing, she thought of Flannery O'Connor's Misfit. Someone comically menacing. A feckless, sinister, ridiculous man.

But that was many months later. At first, the Grifter was seldom seen and rarely spoken of, slipping in and out of the grandmother's house like a shade.

The grandmother had found herself some help, is all she would say. She remained fiercely independent, ferociously private. The grandmother was also oddly content, a warning sign her family missed.

ONE DAY, THE GRANDDAUGHTER came by on her lunch hour unannounced and found the grandmother cooking a feast. Corn bread, fried chicken, okra, sliced cantaloup. There was something proprietary and sly about the way the grandmother stirred the corn bread batter that made the granddaughter feel as if she were intruding. As indeed she was. The dinner was for the man the grandmother had hired, who worked so hard for her, with her. When he was expected, she would not say. She did not invite the granddaughter to stay.

The Grifter had no family. He was dying of cancer. He needed the work. That's what he said, what the grandmother believed.

He was a born-again Christian, he wanted her to read Scripture to him, he needed her. That's what the grandmother believed, what she didn't say.

The grandmother didn't know the Grifter was shrewd, as insidious as a computer virus—malware that infects hardware, cripples networks, siphons bank accounts. He breached the grandmother's hard wall of facts, her brittle judgment, her frugality, by finding a wormhole: her trapdoor for passion, the passion of Christ. For the grandmother had begun to conflate her faith with ecstatic release. When the Grifter, after raking leaves, asked her to pray with him, the grandmother's pent-up fervor filled her like the whistling steam in her pressure cooker. When he asked her to read from Scripture, she took down the Bible from her bookshelf, began her singsong lamenting and reciting, her eyes damp and bright, his hot, calloused hands on her parchment-thin skin. The grandmother believed he loved her to read Scripture—he loved *her*.

It was as if that child inside her from long ago, wanting *more, more, more,* denied for seven decades, awoke again. Yearning seized her. She did not have the will or the strength to deny that child's voice anymore. Nor should she, for the grandmother began to tell herself the child inside her was no longer the voice of sin, but of redemption—his redemption. How she longed for it! She was saving the Grifter, saving his soul, opening his heart.

THE GRIFTER BEGAN TO CALL the grandmother more and more, sobbing. Would she pray for him? With him? She did, weeping too. Once unstoppered, her emotions gushed, difficult to contain. The child's voice inside the grandmother grew louder, once again clamoring for *all the pretty things,* and could not be stemmed. It was only natural that after their Bible lessons, the grandmother and the Grifter went shopping. To Wal-Mart, where the grandmother bought the Grifter clothes, electronics, gift cards. To Red Lobster, where the grandmother treated him to lunch before a stop at the pool and sauna store to order his hot tub. To the bank, where the grandmother withdrew cash, for he needed it to buy his medicine, and he promised to pay back the money she loaned him, a hundred here, a thousand there.

How wonderful to feel so needed, so alive! The grandmother dressed up often, splendid in a pink suit, kitten heels, pearls, and rubies.

The family asked the grandmother to dinner, but she demurred, announced she was having lunch *with a friend,* not that it was any of their business.

But soon it was their business.

THE GRANDMOTHER REFUSED TO TALK about her bank account. When her family asked about it, she grew outraged. The grandmother drove to the bank and gave the twenty-seven-year-old assistant branch manager a dressing down, a public humiliation in the lobby for talking about her "bills" to her family, threatening to take her money elsewhere. I know what I am doing, the grandmother told the bank manager over and over, as he cowered behind his desk.

Sometimes she wasn't home when her grandchildren visited, and she would not say where she was going, where she had been. It was as if the grandmother had turned into a teenager, sneaking off to see a troublesome suitor, and the grandchildren found themselves playing the roles of indignant, furious parents. Was she in love? The granddaughter recalled the reckless intoxication of her first crush at thirteen, like heroin, warm and wonderful in her veins, as the world fell away, as her life narrowed, thin as a straw, and at the end of it, the boy, the beloved. Her straight-A average plummeted, and yet she pined away, offering up her sterling academic record as a sacrifice. It did not matter, her family did not matter, her friends did not matter. Nothing mattered but him, him, him.

One day, a grandson disabled the grandmother's car so she could not drive to meet the Grifter. The grandmother, who took great pride in her robust health, walked three miles to a drugstore to meet him instead.

THE FAMILY PLANNED AN INTERVENTION. There in the grandmother's living room sat a sheriff's deputy, the grandmother's children, her sisters, her grandchildren, great-grandchildren, nieces and nephews. The family never gathered without food. Hence, casseroles and pound cake covered the grandmother's kitchen table. But no one, other than the deputy, had an appetite. The grandmother's family, one by one, began to tell her how frightened they were of this man, the Grifter. Her sister cried and said, Any day I'm going to open the newspaper and read how you've been violated and killed by that no-count criminal you took up with.

The grandmother sat uneasy in her easy chair, her spine erect, her face curiously blank, until fury began to glint in her topaz eyes.

The deputy told the grandmother, told everyone, the Grifter had served time for possession and distribution of drugs, illegal firearms, and on and on. Also, he had an outstanding warrant, and they were going after the son-of-a-bitch. The deputy said the Grifter was a liar, that he did not have cancer, that he drew a disability check because he was an *addict*—some country, huh?

The deputy asked today's date, the grandmother knew it. He gave her a long column of numbers to add. She totaled them quickly as a calculator.

The deputy failed to see the grandmother's mail-slot mouth harden, her face burning with rage, her pride strangling her like a fist as he told her she was being *taken*, that the Grifter preyed on her because she was *elderly and gullible*. The grandmother did not talk or cry, much less admit the Grifter was a criminal. The deputy grew frustrated, everyone grew anxious, because the grandmother would not promise to stop talking to the Grifter.

THE GRANDMOTHER MADE ONE CONCESSION: she would go to the doctor. A check-up with a new family doctor, as the grandmother's previous physician had died of old age. The grandmother took no medicines, her vital signs were healthy, her lab work perfect. The grandmother's vigor impressed the doctor. Keep doing what you're doing, the doctor said.

She is lucid and capable, the doctor said, she can manage her own affairs.

What the family was afraid he would say.

THE DEPUTY ARRESTED THE GRIFTER.

The prosecutor had a caseload of two hundred, but she made time to meet with the grandmother about the upcoming trial. The prosecutor wanted to put the Grifter away for what he did, for what he might do to others. Thirteen thousand dollars gone in as many weeks, plus the grandmother's burial fund.

The prosecutor said the Grifter would not stay behind bars unless the grandmother helped convict him.

The grandmother said, I'm not going to have to get up there on the stand, am I?

Yes, ma'am. You will need to testify.

The grandmother said she would not do it. She began to shake and pressed a tissue to her eyes.

The prosecutor said, Can I be completely frank here? He wants to postpone the trial because he is hoping you will *pass away*. That's what he said.

This did not phase the grandmother. Revenge did not motivate her. Revenge required admitting she'd been foolish, conceding the Grifter had deceived her. The grandmother had no room for vengeance, as shame consumed her. She feared confessing *up there* on the stand as her family listened, as strangers and the Grifter stared.

The grandmother was clever enough to tell the prosecutor she had helped a sinner because she was a good Christian. The grandmother said she knew what she was doing.

The prosecutor closed her eyes for a minute, collecting herself. If the grandmother claimed the money was charity, a gift freely given—the case was over.

The prosecutor said, you are a good person, and he took advantage of that. He is taking advantage of you now. He thinks you won't testify against him. You can't let him win!

The prosecutor told the grandmother her own mother just moved into a retirement village, and it was not a nursing home, no one wants to go to a nursing home, this was about living independently. No upkeep or broken things to fix. Gated and safe.

The grandmother said she had decided long ago where she would live and die—in her own home. She was not leaving it. Ever.

Right now, he can't contact you because he would be in contempt of court if he did, the prosecutor continued. But if I dismiss this, he will contact you. I've been at this job twenty years. I'm willing to bet the Florida State-Clemson game on it, and I'm a big Clemson fan. He will be at your door again. But if you testify—

The grandmother interrupted the prosecutor. She said, I'm not doing it. I will not get up there and testify. I'll go to pieces. I'll die. I will kill myself first.

And that was that.

AFTER MEETING WITH THE PROSECUTOR, the family took the grandmother to lunch. There would be no trial, no testifying. The family was glum, the grandmother giddy with relief. The grandmother ordered a grilled cheese sandwich and iced tea and boxed up her leftover potato chips. Then the grandmother found her lipstick at the bottom of her purse. Her lips were fuchsia, her cheeks rouged, and she smiled. She did not see why the family worried. She wanted to go home, to be left alone.

But within days, the grandmother took ill. Her vision dimmed, her eyesight failed—as if she had willed blindness as punishment, as if her myopia about the Grifter metastasized. She did not drive or cook. When the family hired helpers, the grandmother yelled that strangers were in her house.

She grew dizzy, unsteady, and fell. The grandmother's doctor diagnosed macular degeneration and a fractured wrist.

Her family arranged for the grandmother to move into an assisted living community, Shepherd's Flock. They did not tell the grandmother. They tried, but the grandmother threw a candlestick at them.

ONE DAY, THE GRANDMOTHER'S CHILDREN drove her to Shepherd's Flock. They had secretly furnished her room with the grandmother's prized possessions, her bureau and upholstered chairs, her quilts and potted plants, and though she could no longer read, her bookshelf with the King James Bible, atlas and encyclopedias, her medical dictionary— bookmarked at *diseases of the eye,* which the grandmother had studied with a magnifying glass. They brought in dozens of framed photographs—of the grandmother's husband, her children, her grandchildren and great-grandchildren. The grandmother's room at the assisted living reminded the granddaughter of a college dorm room, artificially cozy to ward away debilitating homesickness.

Then a nurse came by to welcome the grandmother to her new home, where she would be happy now, with three hot meals every day, prayer services, Bingo, ceramics and crafts, and so many new friends to make. The grandmother exploded. She screamed she had been tricked. She demanded to leave, to be taken home. She took down the photographs of her family and threw them in her sock drawer. She did not eat for days, refused to get out of bed, had to be diapered. For a week this went on, then two.

When her children came to pray with her, she closed her eyes and told them they were evil demons, she hated them.

The grandmother did not want to live, but she was too angry to die.

THEN, A MIRACLE. That was what the nursing aide called it. A month later, the grandmother began, quite suddenly, to recover. She ate with the appetite of a farmhand, and she took a keen interest in physical therapy.

The grandmother walked in the hallways with a cane, no more wheelchair. She allowed her hair to be washed and styled, her nails painted. Her strength rebounded, her stamina inextinguishable. Her doctors were impressed. Keep doing what you're doing, they told her.

Her blindness lifted. Or so she claimed. I have prayed on it, she said, and I am going to get my eyes seeing again. She told her granddaughter she was leaving that place. The grandmother had willed her decline; she would will her recovery. Soon I will be strong enough, the grandmother said. I am going home. You don't believe me? I will walk out of here, I will walk every step of the way to my house. I will.

It is what she said a year later in that place, and every year since. When she turned one hundred, the grandmother refused to blow out candles on her cake. She would bake her *own* cake, in her *own* kitchen, in her *own* house. Just you wait.

MINDY FRIDDLE'S short stories have appeared in *storySouth, LitMag, Hayden's Ferry Review, Southern Humanities Review, Orca, Sinking City, Blood & Bourbon, Gateway Review*, and other journals. She is the author of the novels *The Garden Angel*, selected for Barnes and Noble's Discover Great New Writers program, and *Secret Keepers*, winner of the Willie Morris Award for Southern Fiction. Mindy's third novel, *Her Best Self*, is forthcoming in 2024. She lives on Edisto Island, in South Carolina.

Heartworms
Robert Busby

ALL THE BOY WANTED WAS A GUN to put his dog out of its misery. His grandfather had told him once that most of God's creatures were not made to suffer. Most of God's creatures included gut-shot deer and broke-leg horses and terminal cases of most dog breeds. Chad, 11, owned a dog that was one of those breeds, a rat terrier that he had received for his second Christmas. Now the worms in its heart had retreated to the creature's lungs, where they swelled her black-brown-spotted white fur like a helium nozzle had been stuck up her poor pink ass.

Chad had his fingers locked into chain links in the fence. His forehead rested against the patterned metal and a pentagon had been dented into its thin flesh. Most of the afternoon had been burned away watching Lady struggle to her feet, wobble across the pallet of pine needles covering the pen, and whimper at the boy's high tops. She started with a cough of some persistence a couple of months ago. Then sacrifices of blind, gnawed-at moles that she would dig up around the yard were no longer left on the back stoop of their house. Sprints toward realms unknown ceased.

"Just gettin old," his old man had said.

But this week had been when her belly had swelled. And then kept on swelling, her fur stretched taut around her ribcage, her backbone defined as knuckles.

"Heart-damn-worms," he said. "Nothin' we can do about it. Not a damn thing."

Today was Saturday. First official day of spring break. First thing this morning the boy had unlatched the gate and offered Lady the chance to run around. The dog would have none of it. The boy changed out her water and gave her fresh dry food. But all day he avoided touching her, resisted scratching her fur behind her unclipped ears and her hind leg. She stared up at him with eyes that could not comprehend his betrayal. But he could not push past the thought that she might explode heartworms all over him.

The sun flattened out across the horizon. Inside he found his old man dozing in the blue corduroy recliner, the footrest kicked up, a sitcom muted on the television. He was a small-shouldered man and thin except for a small paunch of gut his unbuttoned jeans accommodated. A Mountain Dew sweated onto the end table. The laminate surface curled away from one of the corners and a Gulfport coaster sat next to the can.

He nudged his old man's shoulder. "Pops."

He watched his father's slack-jawed, stubbled chin work its mouth into words. "Huh."

"Was wondering," the boy said.

"Some Dinty Moore in the cabinet you can heat up." His old man thumped the Mountain Dew can. The can rang hollow. "Get me another Dew."

The boy went to the kitchen. "They ain't any in the fridge."

"Try the one in the garage."

There Mountain Dews shared space with his mother's Old Milwaukees. Cans of either divided the shelves and filled the storage in the doors. Chad took a Mountain Dew back to his father. His father cracked it open, drained a good bit of it, and flipped some channels on the television. Taxidermy flew feathered around the living room and a deer peered its antlered noggin out from the wood-paneled walls. His father did not hunt now, and Chad had no interest in the sport except for the evidence that his father had shot a gun before and may still have that gun somewhere in the house.

"Pops."

"Huh."

"Was wondering if you could teach me how to hunt?"

"Hunt what?"

"Deer I guess."

"Too late this season."

"What's in season?"

"Work's got me too busy anyway."

"Can teach myself then if you just get me a gun."

His father pulled on the Mountain Dew again then produced a can of Grizzly from his back pocket. He packed the can against his palm before he snatched a plug that he folded impressively quick into his lip, spitting some strands of the snuff from his lip into the empty can.

"What's the sudden interest?"

Chad betrayed his intentions by looking towards the backyard.

"This got anything to do with that dog of yours?"

"Sir?"

"Listen to me. Leave that dog alone. I ain't got time this week to dig a grave."

"But she won't run around or dig up moles. We should of took her to Dr. Svens."

"Ain't gonna pay a vet for something I can handle by my damn self."

THAT NIGHT CHAD SPOONED MICROWAVED beef stew and watched his father snore from the recliner until he was convinced he was out until morning. His mother was at the hospital. She worked a twelve-hour shift on Saturdays and two other days during the week. Chad snuck through their bedroom into the closet. He looked around and behind his parents' clothes. Chad had a perfectly fine air rifle his grandfather had left on their doorstep last year for his birthday. He knew little about guns except that he needed something that could do more than fart out BBs.

At the bottom of one of the drawers he did find what he had learned from a classmate's creased Playboy was a thong. That find surprised him. He had known for about a year now from locker-room talk in P.E. how he had been conceived in a sort of general sense, but Chad could not remember a night his father had not fallen asleep on the recliner and not still been there snoring the next morning. But there must have been at least one time when his old man felt inspired enough to peel himself off the recliner and visit Chad's mother in bed. Or perhaps she had taken the initiative, put on this thong, and met him on that ratty old corduroy recliner just once.

An hour later he concluded his search and that, if his father still possessed a rifle or a shotgun, he kept it locked up and dormant as his pecker.

THE NEXT DAY WAS SUNDAY and church and pan-fried pork afterwards at his grandparents' house. His grandparents lived in a small rancher on three acres on the outskirts of Bodock. Along the east end of the property was the railroad that his grandfather Hambone had worked for. Between the house and the tracks sat the barn with its thin fiberglass walls where horses were raised and shod and broken to subsidize his earnings at the rail yard. When Hambone was made supervisor, he continued the side enterprise out of habit and hobby.

In the kitchen Granny slipped the last batch of thin battered chops into the skillet on the stove. The chops rejoiced when they hit that hot grease. Hambone rode into the dining room from the den, his six-foot-five frame hunched over the motorized scooter. He wore a polyester button down and light starched khakis and a hem of the khakis caught on the mouth of a work boot. He shook Chad's hand again like he had in the fellowship hall lounge at the Methodist church in front of all the other old timers and coffee drinkers. His paw swallowed Chad's and whipped his thin arm around like a horse would its tail.

At the table were deviled eggs, mashed potatoes, and brown gravy. On a plate lined with paper towels, fried chops spread their grease like slick colorless blood. The way Granny's bony fingers clutched the hardboiled egg half when she served Chad reminded him of Lady's rib cage stretched out across her firm swollen belly.

"Eat up boy," Hambone said. "Chad here's puny as a rail pin. Y'all ain't feeding him?"

"He gets fed, Pops," Chad's father said. He wore khakis and a casual khaki wind jacket over a polo shirt and sat next to Granny, holding a plastic bottle of Mountain Dew. Chad's mother was at home. She had slept in that morning after leaving five empty beer cans on the counter after her shift.

"Don't seem y'all are doing a good job of fattening up this foal."

"Got a high metabolism I guess."

"Hell. He's about to hit the spurt and his bones ain't got any fat to stretch with."

About all of Chad's classmates at school had hit the spurt, so to speak, and had filled out, but Chad was still waiting for his turn.

After lunch Hambone excused himself to digest his food lying down.

Granny slurped coffee while she cleared the table and washed the dishes.

"Billy wants to know if Chad can sit with him tomorrow," she said.

Chad's father had moved from the table to a stool near the counter and spit into the emptied Mountain Dew bottle before twisting the green cap back on. "What for?"

"I don't know. He's got to sit in this dusty house alone while I work. He can't get around anywhere or drive. Ain't got any neighbors but them blacks now. He likes to spend his days out in the barn, but he can't get there and then inside all by himself. Needs someone to hold the door so he can drive up and down the ramp. Think it might be good to have Chad around during the day, get his mind off wondering when his next heart attack gonna come."

His father removed the cap again and spat twice into the bottle before twisting the cap back on. "What if something happens?"

"He ain't like he was with you. He don't drink no more."

"Meant like a heart attack."

"I gotta take a leak," Chad said to no one.

Hambone was occupying the hall bathroom, but Chad didn't really have to go anyway. Was just worried about being here tomorrow. Chad knew to call 911 if Hambone had a heart attack but didn't know what one looked like. But it wasn't just that. His father had often joked about getting his ass whipped with a limb from the bodock in the backyard until his legs bled. Chad's own father had only ever popped him with his hand a couple of times. That never hurt much.

Chad wandered past the hall bathroom but stopped when he got to the open door to his grandparents' bedroom at the end of the hall. The maroon comforter on the king bed was faded and stained and turned back from depressed pillows. Chunky blue carpet on the floor. A wheelchair Hambone had abandoned for the scooter leaned folded in a corner and the walker he had not managed for some time stood beside a nightstand covered with papers and torn-open envelopes and a Bible. A handgun of some caliber weighed down a stack of papers.

Chad hung his head back out the doorjamb and looked down the hallway to the kitchen. Could still hear them talking. Hambone still in the bathroom. He thought he had enough time to catch a quick glimpse of the gun. Even had the thought he could pocket it before Hambone got out of the bathroom. But he had no clue what kind of gun that was, if it'd be any account in ending Lady's misery. Or if there was a better gun to use. He walked quickly over to it. Its metal was black, and it had a wood-grained handle. He reached out his hand then paused. Still heard no movement. He recognized the design as a revolver because of westerns and the spinning chamber. The revolver surprised him with its heft. He imagined such a heavy gun would do the trick. Tried not to imagine the blood that would spread like oil or grease, the pine straw soaking it up like paper towels.

"That's a Colt .45"

Chad jerked at the voice that boomed behind him. He dropped the Colt on the ground.

"Careful there, boy." Hambone drove the scooter around the bed. Chad had never appreciated how quiet the machine whispered along on its battery power until now that it had snuck up on him. Hambone bent over to retrieve the Colt. The waft of Old Spice and sweat and the rot of Hambone's labored breath reached Chad. In the last half decade Hambone had suffered three heart attacks and an open-heart surgery. Had a hip replaced with an artificial one. Slipped some discs and had the operations to fix them. Still, he had a head full of gray hair greased into a part. Hambone said, "Damn good way to blow your ankle clean off your foot. Good thing it ain't loaded though."

Some dust motes floated about. Hambone stooped over in the chair, inspecting the revolver and then Chad. Mumbled something to himself. He seemed to be going over an important thing in his mind and did not speak for a few minutes. Chad feared his grandfather was contemplating whether he would report Chad. His father would put this together with his warning last night and would perhaps hire Hambone to administer a bodock limb continuously across his ass.

"My son ain't never taught you about guns?"

"No sir."

"About how to shoot?"

"No sir."

"Hell then. Let's learn you how."

CHAD WAS DROPPED OFF JUST BEFORE eight the next morning. Granny had already left to calculate her teller drawer at the Peoples Bank. His father had lost the argument with his mother that evening about dropping Chad off. He was running late to work now and didn't walk Chad to the door. Chad hung around on the stoop of the carport before he mustered the courage to go in. Inside, he walked by the washer and dryer in the mudroom into the kitchen that opened into the dining room. The scooter was pulled up parallel to the dining table and Hambone sat sideways in the seat eating leftover fried pork chops and biscuits Granny woke up early to knead.

"Help yourself," Hambone said. Chad cut open a biscuit over a clean plate and buttered one side of the biscuit and then the other after Hambone told him he needed to fatten up some. Scooped some Welch's grape jelly onto his biscuit with a spoon left in the plastic jar. Over the jelly he placed two slices of cheese already carved out of the wheel of red wax and slapped a fried pork chop between the dressed biscuit.

Chad walked the plate over to the table. He was not used to having company when he ate. Most mornings he sat on the couch and spooned Fruit Loops or Golden Grahams or ate pancake and sausage on a stick, a breakfast version of a corn dog that came frozen in a Jimmy Dean box. He could never get the sausage fully thawed in the microwave. The pork was cold, but Hambone said that was the only way to eat anything that had been fried and leftover. Hambone wore worked-in khakis and a clean button-down white shirt, stained brown around the collar with long-ago sweat. The shirt had short sleeves and his rail-tie forearms held liver spots. A gold medical bracelet on his wrist. He slurped at his steaming coffee.

"You want some coffee?"

Chad shrugged. "Never had any before."

"Gonna be a day of firsts for you. There's a cup hanging on a peg over the Bunn over there. Pour you some whole milk in the cup first then the coffee. Stir in some sugar after that."

After breakfast Hambone retrieved the gun from the bedroom and brought it and a holster to the kitchen. The gun closet, which had originally been intended as a pantry, was the first door on the right off the dining room.

Hambone jiggled the handle. "Shit. Granny done locked it again."

Chad tongued at a hunk of pork caught between molars. "Where's the key?"

"Don't know."

"Where's the last place you had it?"

"Knew that then the damn thing wouldn't be lost."

Chad shrugged. "That's what my mom always asks when I lose something."

"Sounds like something her drunk ass would say."

Chad didn't know how to respond. It was true that she often said those exact words with an Old Milwaukee in her hand or her head still under a pillow come lunchtime and Chad in need or want of something.

"All right. Another lesson. No matter who it is or whether their opinion's valid, anyone ever say something like that about your mother you punch them in the goddamn face. Understood?"

Chad nodded and cornered the pork abrasion against his gums.

"You know how to throw a punch?"

Chad shook his head. "No sir."

"I'll learn you that another day. Hell. Where's that goddamn key."

Chad dislodged the pork in his teeth. With nowhere to spit, he was forced to swallow it. He had the thought that they would get nowhere today without a key and felt like kicking the door down. He looked at the small round hole in the doorknob. They made slender keys for it, but such a key wasn't necessary to open it.

"Hambone," Chad said. "I can get this door unlocked."

"How?"

"Need a coat hanger."

Hambone squinted an eye at the possibility. "There's some empty ones in that back bedroom."

Chad retrieved a hanger out of a closet of the retired bedroom. Cobwebs coated the corners of the room. A large spider crawled across the ceiling. The pillowcases were brown and dirty. Chad retrieved a hanger and carried it back down the hall, unwrapping the coiled neck into a straight rod before inserting the straighter end into the hole. He fiddled the hanger around until he had located the lever to the lock, which he depressed and held down while he twisted the doorknob. The door creaked open.

"Well sumbitch," Hambone said out the side of an impressed smirk. The closet proved too small for both of them, so he pointed Chad's attention toward the popcorn ceiling. "The cartridges gonna be up there in one of them boxes on the top shelf. There's a step stool right there."

The closet held all kinds of old guns coated in varying degrees of dust that spoke of the duration of their disuse. Longer guns were braced upright against the wall. Some wide barreled and narrow ones and some of the narrow barrels held scopes. Lined on the lower shelf were pistols. Like cousins they resembled the one Hambone kept on his nightstand. Chad climbed to the top shelf and chose a box and reached it down for his grandfather to inspect.

"Dust off the box," Hambone said. So Chad did. Dust motes snowed toward the carpet. Hambone waved the air clear in front of his face and said, "Nah. Them are twenty-two cartridges. Get the box next to 'em down."

Chad returned the box to its dustless indentation among the exoskeletons of long dried-out insect carcasses littering the shelf. He wondered how Hambone got the bullets down on his own when the door was unlocked. Chad chose the correct box next and when he stepped off the stool he pointed at the longest of the thin barreled guns. The breech of the gun held some kind of cool scope. "Kind of gun is that?"

"Two-seventy."

"What about that one?"

"Twelve gauge."

"What's a twelve gauge?"

"A shotgun."

"What about the two-seventy?"

"A rifle."

"What's the difference?"

"One has a rifled barrel. Spins the bullet around, makes it travel further. Don't explode until on impact." Hambone mimicked the flight of a rifle cartridge by spinning the index finger of one hand toward Chad. When the index finger reached his grandson's chest Hambone demonstrated the detonation of the cartridge by spreading all of his fingers out. "The other fires shells filled with metal bearings. Ain't got the range of a rifle, but the shells explode when fired and the bearings spread out as they're discharged and cover a wider target at a closer distance."

This time Hambone positioned his fingers like a shadow puppet, slowly spreading out his palm and fingers as he moved his hand toward Chad. "You can use either hunting. The shotgun's good for killing ducks and birds, small game like rabbits and squirrels. A twenty-two rifle is good for rabbits and squirrels also. Can still use a shotgun for deer. Use birdshot for winged game and buckshot for hunting deer."

"What's birdshot and buckshot?"

Chad thought he might be asking too many questions, the coffee coursing through him, turning him jittery and hyper. But Hambone didn't seem annoyed. He rested his arms on the handlebars of the scooter and explained how birdshot-grade bearings were smaller than buckshot-grade bearings so they didn't fuck up the bird meat so much you couldn't eat it.

"Could use a slug in the shotgun as well," Hambone said. Chad started to ask what a slug was, but Hambone went on: "Ought to get on down to the barn to shoot. Fixin' to burn away the rest of our day up here." Hambone mulled over something else and said, "Climb back up there and get the box of twelve-gauge birdshot. The two-seventy might go right through the barn, hit one of the blacks over in the project down there. But we can give the twelve gauge a try. Hopefully it ain't gonna kick the joint right out of that scrawny shoulder of yours."

ON THE WAY TO THE BACKYARD Chad walked in front of the scooter. In a plastic Jitney Jungle grocery bag, he collected horse apples from the bodock tree littering the path so Hambone's scooter did not run up on one. They also needed the horse apples to shoot at. Hambone carried the pistol on his hip in the worn leather holster and the box of rounds in the cage affixed to the handlebars. The shotgun he cradled in the nook of his elbow. With his free hand he steered the scooter out to the backside of the barn in the bright sunlight. The battery-quiet motor like a sustained muffled fart. The sun had not yet burned off the morning chill.

"Go in the barn there and bring out some bales," Hambone said.

"How many?"

"However many you can bring out here until I say you ain't got to bring no more."

The hay was wet and molded and the rope holding each bale cut through the hay, spilling it on the dirt floor. Chad had to manage one bale at a time, which he heaved onto the ground against the exterior wall at the back of the barn. Once Chad had seen his grandfather hurl a damn horse right out of that barn. Not a pony. A full-grown walking horse too stubborn or not broken enough to yield to a bit. Hambone grabbed the horse around its neck and whipped the equine mass around, sent it stumbling to the dirt of the pen adjoining the barn. After the family had all left that afternoon, Hambone broke the horse's leg while trying to break its spirit down enough to follow his orders and had to put the beast down. Hambone himself couldn't ride a horse anymore and had sold them all off because he couldn't even tend to them. Sure as hell couldn't toss one onto the ground now. Chad wondered whether Hambone would have already put his own self down like he had the walking horse that afternoon. But folks were different than animals.

When Chad had amassed ten bales, Hambone instructed him to build two stacks of four bales horizontally against the barn as a buffer so the bullets could not travel through the thin fiberglass wall. He stood two more bales in front of those stacks. On the shorter stack he placed three bodock balls from the plastic bag.

Hambone had parked the scooter about fifteen feet from the barn. There he showed Chad how to load the gun. He switched off the safety and flipped the safety latch that allowed the barreled magazine to swing away from the hammer and barrel. Hambone slipped a single bullet into one of the six holes in the round magazine. He handed the gun to Chad to load.

Hambone said, "The tapered end of the round should point away from you in the same direction as you'd be aiming."

Chad held the gun with his right hand while he filled the rest of the empty chambers with his left. He returned the gun to Hambone and Hambone showed his grandson how to cock the hammer, how to line up the sight at the end of the muzzle between the two sights over the breech. Hambone held the gun with both hands, saddled the scooter sideways, and allowed himself about a second to aim. The bullet tore through the horse apple on the far left. A section of the horse apple axed from the whole.

"Your turn," Hambone said.

In his effort to draw back the stubborn hammer Chad accidentally pulled the trigger. The pistol cracked loudly and surprised him as spat dirt up from the ground in front of them. The pistol nearly kicked out of his hand.

"Keep your finger off the trigger until you're ready to fire."

Chad's first shot missed the hay bales completely and drew a hole in the side of the barn. Later, when he was returning the hay bales, he would notice the dot of light on the dirt floor, its tail following to the hole in the thin wall that already filtered daylight like translucent membrane. His next two shots landed in the short stack of hay bales. His sixth and final round grazed one of the horse apples, shaved off some yellow ridges, and spun the ball on the bale.

"All right. Not terrible. Reload and try again."

By the fourth shot of the second reload Chad had solidly nailed one of the horse apples, which exploded into thirds.

AT TWELVE THEY RETIRED THE HAY BALES to the barn. Chad raked up straw that had fallen out of the bales then collected the horse apple fragments, forty-five casings, and emptied twelve-gauge shells in the Jitney Jungle bag, which he chunked over the chain-link fence into the railyard like Hambone instructed.

Before preparing lunch, they put away the Colt and the twelve gauge. Chad's shoulder was still sore from the recoil of the shotgun. The first shot had kicked him to the ground. After the second round his shoulder had felt like it would about dislocate. While Hambone drove down the hall to return the Colt to his nightstand, Chad climbed the foot stool and realized he did not have the box of forty-five cartridges. When Hambone returned Chad glanced at the empty basket on the handlebars and asked if Hambone had the cartridges.

"Think I might of left 'em in the barn."

"You need me to go get 'em?"

"Nah. We can get 'em tomorrow. About to get some lunch right now. You done wore me out."

The cartridges down at the barn might have made for easy picking but there was no way to borrow the Colt without Hambone realizing it was gone. There was a whole closet of other guns here but no way for Chad to know which one to try to sneak out.

Before Hambone could reverse out of the gun closet Chad asked, "What if you need to put an animal out of its misery? What kind is best then?"

Hambone stopped to consider the question. "A handgun. Something small like a twenty-two."

Chad said, "I thought those was a rifle."

"They make 'em in revolvers too. Use the same long-range cartridges as the rifle."

Hambone waved Chad out of the closet so he could a pistol smaller than the Colt .45 from the lower shelf. "There's a twenty-two."

Chad took the pistol from Hambone's paw. "Can I have it?"

Hambone considered it. "You ain't quite ready to have a gun on your own. 'Specially not in town limits." He handed the gun to Chad despite his words. The revolver was much lighter than the Colt, but the magazine mechanisms and hammer were similar.

"Hide it in your room," Hambone said. "Practice releasing the magazine and cocking the hammer. Clean it some. It's a good starter pistol."

"How do I clean it?"

"I'll show you after lunch."

"What about bullets?"

"Some wishful thinking there. But hell no."

For an hour after a lunch of store-bought pimento cheese sandwiches, Hambone taught Chad how to load and unload the twenty-two revolver with empty twenty-two shells that had already been discharged. When they were finished, Chad stowed away the twenty-two and the empty shells at the bottom of his backpack and the rest of the afternoon was burned away sitting in the den. Only a little daylight came through the window curtains. John Wayne howdy-partnering and hello-pilgrimming on the television.

Chad listened for several minutes after Hambone began snoring upright in the recliner. Then he retrieved the hanger again from the spare bedroom and picked the lock on the gun closet. Quietly he grabbed a handful of live twenty-two rounds from the dust-streaked box on the top shelf and packed those in his bag as well.

HIS MOM WAS ON A SHIFT that evening and Pops was passed out on the couch. Chad went to his room and raised his shirt up in the tall mirror on the back of his bedroom door to inspect the proud bruise on his shoulder. He unpacked his bag, pulled the twenty-two from the bottom and the empty and live cartridges, and hid the empty ones in his closet in the pocket of an old winter coat he had outgrown where they clanked against a half-empty can of his father's snuff he was still mustering the courage to try.

He fed the live rounds into the revolver and walked out to the dog pen. The gun was heavier loaded and gave him a sense of power that quickened his heart rate and unsettled his stomach. Lady lay halfway out of her doghouse. Chad found himself praying she had just died already. She struggled to her feet though when she heard him at the gate, her lungs wheezing as she hobbled toward him. The gate rattled the chain link behind him. He hid the twenty-two behind his back and took a knee in the moist pine needles.

"Hey girl," he said. The fence around their yard was chain-linked as well. Some neighbors had left their porch lights on, but no one was out to watch. With his left hand he began to search her head and neck for some tender efficient spot that would accept the bullet with the least pain. When he groped behind her floppy unclipped ears, her hind leg kicked lazily at her swollen side. He rubbed behind her ear some more. Her leg nudged her flank again and she whimpered yearnings for him to continue. He massaged her head and muzzle, the tips of her floppy unclipped ears. Her leg was out of control. Chad laughed and kept at it until he realized he could not do this tonight. He imagined her head detonating as the horse apples had and that sounded pretty damn awful. He told himself a bullet in her neck or lungs or heart would just hurt her more.

Chad caught a stank of shit. Somewhere in the pen was a steaming turd pile and the motion sensor floodlight on the back of the house did not light up the pen enough to risk finding and cleaning it up without smashing it beneath his shoes or the knee of his jeans. The worms had been making her constipated so he decided this was a sign, a bill of improving health. He decided she would sleep in his room tonight. On the floor instead of the bed though, in the event she exploded heartworms.

IN THE MORNING, a knock on his bedroom door awoke him. His father leaned in wearing a National Furniture t-shirt tucked into his blue jeans and an unbuttoned flannel shirt. White tennis shoes beneath the tapered cuff of his jeans. Lady raised her head.

"What's the dog doing in here?"

"I dunno." Chad found the remote on his nightstand and turned on the television. Tom and Jerry quietly beat the shit out of each other.

His father furrowed his brow at the dog's wheezing. "She don't look so good. Came down here to tell you Granny called on her way out the door. Said Hambone was still worn out from yesterday and was taking a raincheck on today."

Chad scratched biscuits and fried pork or bacon off his wish list and would have to settle for the bowl of Fruit Loops waiting on him upstairs. Pops said, "About to go into work. Need anything?" Chad shook his head. He had slept in his white briefs and was waiting for his father to leave before he crawled out of bed to throw on his jeans and a shirt. Pops made to turn then stopped, looking back at Chad. "Where the hell you get that bruise?"

Chad forced his eyes to stick to the television, fixed on Tom chasing Jerry with a wooden mallet. "Uh, what bruise?"

"Don't play dumb. The damn bruise on your shoulder."

Chad looked at his shoulder. Thought, Shit. Kept staring at his shoulder long enough for Tom to get his tail clamped in a mouse trap and three knots somehow pounded on his own head with his own mallet.

"Dunno."

"To hell with that. Hambone grab you?"

"No."

"He hit you?"

"No!"

Pops inhaled deeply and grabbed Chad hard by the shoulders as if trying to squeeze the answer out of him. He let go when he saw Chad wince at the bruise caught in his father's grip. He walked out of the room to the phone in the hallway. Chad could hear him speaking to himself through an intermittent series of rings, saying comeoncomeoncomeon. His father came back in the room. "Hambone ain't answering. Get dressed."

"Why?"

"'Cause I fucking said. Let Lady out then meet me at the truck."

HIS FATHER PEELED THE TIRES of the Ford Ranger off Main Street onto Gatlin Road. Antebellum homes suffering peeling paint and sagging foundations and other states of disrepair flanked either side of the street before easing into what his father called the ghetto, a government project of identical detached homes, squat brick structures enclosed in chain link fencing that encroached on the north end of Hambone's property.

His father's tires spit gravel like flakes of snuff when he wheeled into the driveway and braked hard behind Granny's empty space in the carport. He shut off the truck and pocketed the keys and grabbed the empty Mountain Dew can in the cup holder. "Come on. We're gonna have us a little talk with Hambone then I'm gonna take your ass back home and be late for damn work again I guess."

Chad followed his father up the stoop and watched with the helplessness of the convicted as his father banged a fist against the security door. The door was metal and had been spray painted white instead of powder coated. His father banged again, longer this time. The handle to the security door was unlocked and his father opened it and banged against the wood door behind it. No answer. His father stepped back and mulled something over before checking the key ring in his pocket and mumbling Shit to himself. But then he started as if he'd remembered some important thing and found a spare key on the sill of the mudroom window.

"Go wait by the truck."

"What for?"

"Because Hambone ain't answering. Quit asking fucking questions."

"You think Hambone had a heart attack?"

His father ignored him. He unlocked the door and opened it a little. "Stay out here."

If it was a heart attack, Chad was glad it hadn't happened on his watch. He felt sad and hoped Hambone was just laid up in bed. He wanted Hambone able to get around to teaching him more stuff. How to drink coffee. How to throw a punch.

His father wasn't in the house long before Chad remembered the box of bullets Hambone had left down at the barn yesterday. He walked down there and in one of the stalls found Hambone had slid off the scooter. He had been sitting sideways on the scooter and lay flat on his back now in the hay. His legs had caught on the seat and the toes of his work boots pointed upwards. A wall of the stall carried liver spots of blood and the swoop of Hambone's gray hair mopped at the blood that spilled out of the stall. There was too much for the hay to soak it all. Daylight pointed to the spillage through the hole Chad had left in the fiberglass wall of the barn yesterday, the Colt death gripped by paws that had swung rail ties like thin bodock switches. Chad heard his father yelling for him and for Hambone and he thought about Lady's leg in its Christmas ecstasy last night. Hambone's legs were still propped on the seat of the scooter. Legs that weren't broken like the walking horse's but that hadn't been of much more use to Hambone either. Further, Hambone had all those heart attacks. Granny told Pops that Hambone was just waiting until the next one came. Like he was carrying around leaking sticks of dynamite, biding his time until one blew his ass away. A heart full of worms just ready to explode.

ROBERT BUSBY grew up in a small dry town in the hill country of North Mississippi and has worked as a bandsaw operator, a powder coater, a produce clerk, a driving school instructor, a bookseller, and a satellite television technician. His work has appeared in *Arkansas Review, Cold Mountain Review, Flash! Writing the Very Short Story* (Norton), *Mississippi Noir* (Akashic), *PANK, Sou'wester, stymie: a journal of sports & literature*, and *Surreal South* '11 (Press 53). Currently, he's a content strategist in Memphis, TN, where he writes, runs, and raises two humans with his wife.

Last Dance with Mary Jane
C.O. Davidson

Eliot sits on the curb, shivering, despite the humid night, an unopened bag of Funyuns clutched in his hands. Blue lights wash over him. Two county cops stand by their squad cars. Eliot thinks he recognizes one of them. As they talk, their eyes shift to him, then slide back to their notepads, their radios, each other. Then to Eliot again. A silent ambulance pulls into the parking lot.

Somewhere, in the Stop-Rite, in a back room, amid shrink-wrapped pallets of Slim Jims and Corn Nuts, in the glow of a security monitor, cops huddle, reviewing the tape:

CAM 01 / 10/14/94 / 17:34:04

In a wash of video blues and static, in the upper left of the frame, a young girl mixes sodas: 7-up, Mountain Dew, Hi-C Orange.

("A suicide, that's what we called it in my day. When you mix all those different flavors.")

Hip cocked in white jeans, she slides to the left and tops off with Wild Cherry Pepsi. She seals her drink and stabs the top with a straw, relief to the boredom of this night.

Meanwhile, five miles away, in the center of town, the football stadium glows, drawing the rest of her classmates, and their parents, grandparents, cousins, most of the town, all of them wanting to feel connected to something bigger than themselves. *Like Jesus*, she thinks, not knowing she's already a ghost on this tape.

Cut. To before.

Eliot slumps, two desks back from Connie, sixth-period Algebra.

The teacher, Mr. Woodburn, keeps his back to the class most of the hour, his voice bouncing off the blackboard as he gets lost in binomials.

Connie spends much of the class listening to the Caldwell twins. Both cheerleaders, they habitually turn to face her, or each other. It's Friday, and the twins wear their uniforms to class, tight sweaters with CHS stretched across their chests. Pleated skirts fan across tan thighs that flex. Their Buster Browns leave black scuff marks on the linoleum. Connie always wears jeans. Her tennis shoes glow, pristine white, white like nothing in Eliot's closet or in the entire trailer he and his brother, Mark, share.

Eliot watches the clock, the second hand slowing down as he listens to the twins talk about people they know, parties that happened or will happen, all like characters and plots on a television show that Eliot will never watch. He wonders if Connie would watch, or would she change the channel?

BACK PRESSED AGAINST HIS LOCKER, he watches her cut through the crowded hall, gray eyes, pink lips, blonde crimped hair floating over her shoulders. A head taller than many of the boys, she never walks slump-shouldered, is not embarrassed by her height.

She is better than that.

Later that night, stretched out on the narrow bed in his small paneled bedroom, carpet mildewed, the ceiling fan turning and turning and turning until his vision blurs and Connie appears, turning and turning and turning in the hallway at school, looking over her shoulder, seeing him seeing her.

And she smiles.

("REWIND IT, TO EARLIER.") / 10/14/94 / 16:46.13

Center frame: the girl leans over the counter. A tabloid spread before her. It could be a Midnight Sun, *but likely it's* The Enquirer, *known more for celebrities than Bat Boys in caves. Her brows knit, as she draws something—glasses or horns—on a blurry photo of the actor caught in an affair with the family nanny. She looks up to the door, as a man, maybe in his sixties, dressed in overalls, walks in. She puts her hand over her art and smiles at the customer. Professional. But also like she has a secret.*

The man pays for gas, leaves.

Last spring, after a Saturday swim meet, was the first time he saw her.

Per his detention, he had to clean the locker rooms and pick up trash around the stands at the pool.

Chlorine burning his nose, he picks up a wadded paper cup some slob parent dropped, and when he looks up, she's there.

Wearing a red suit, tall and wet and beautiful as a knife, she stands by the pool, toes curling over the edge. Staring across the water. The meet had been over for an hour.

Eliot freezes, clutching the metal trashcan to his chest.

"Fennick!" Coach Wexler yells from his office. "Meet's over!"

She takes two steps back, turns, and walks into the girls' locker room, leaving behind damp prints that fade into the concrete, each curved arch a mysterious note.

"As if," one of the twins says, soon as Woodburn's back turns.

"It's not like he's your real dad," says the other twin.

"All the same," Connie says. "He pays the bills. So what he says goes. For now."

"But a job? On Fridays? The weekends? You'll miss homecoming."

"I'll live," Connie says, suddenly interested in the contents of her Algebra book.

The twins share a look then face forward in their seats.

Two desks back, Eliot can hear their synchronized thoughts: *She's on her own now.*

A week later he sits on the floor in Bound Periodicals, the back row of the library. He balances a thick paperback on his knees as he eats his lunch: bologna and white bread. No drink.

A shadow passes into his periphery. He braces himself for the rebuke, another detention.

"Sorry. Is this aisle taken?"

From down here, she looks even taller: loose blonde hair, letter jacket, jeans, those so-white tennis shoes. He shakes his head.

Connie walks down the aisle and sits a few feet from him, her back against the same shelf as his. She unshoulders and sets her backpack between them. "Didn't realize anyone was back here," she says and unzips her backpack, pulling out a Coke and a Snickers. "Want one?" She pulls out a second candy bar and holds it out to Eliot. "Price of admission? For invading your space?"

"It's okay."

"Go on. I take them from work. Perk of the job."

Eliot takes the candy bar. Their fingers almost touch.

"Thanks."

"How is it?"

"Good," he says, after a bite.

She laughs. "I mean the book. I love King."

"It's good. Even longer than *The Stand*."

"It's about a bunch of kids, right? Probably an asshole father too? He definitely gets those. Not that my dad is swinging any mallets. My *step*-dad."

"Miss Fennick." Mr. Link, the vice-principal, blocks the end of the aisle. Backlit by fluorescent light, his dark suit looks cut from tin. "Just what do the two of you think you're doing in here? Lunch should be eaten in the cafeteria. Not the library."

"A tutoring session. Ms. Thistle said it was okay to meet here. Sir."

Eliot sags against the shelf. Why else would anyone believe Connie Fennick would waste her lunch period? With him.

Link squints at Eliot, mouth forming a hard line instead of the word he wants to say: *Trash.*

A beat.

"Bell's in two minutes. Get to class. I don't want to catch you eating in here again." Link pivots like a clockwork and leaves them.

Connie stands with her Coke and backpack. "Another asshole, right?"

"Yeah."

"See you in class." And then she smiles at him.

And this will be the best day of his life.

("Fast-forward. Stop.") / 0/14/94 / 19:04:08:10

Center frame: she sits behind the cash register, sleeves of her letter jacket pushed up, holding open, one-handed, a fat paperback. From its cover a demonic clown stares out with silver eyes. Her own eyes still on the page, she takes a long pull of soda from a bent straw. Suddenly, she straightens, rolls her eyes, takes a breath, and lets it out. Slowly. She places the book face down on the counter. Looks toward the door. A man walks into frame. Average height. Face turned away from the camera. A bald spot. Glasses. Dark Members Only jacket. She smiles, says . . .

("What is that? What's she saying?")

"Damn. No Audio.")

A glitch in the tape. Snow.

Nothing but snow.

ELIOT WISHES HE HADN'T STOLEN THAT JOINT FROM MARK.

Wishes he hadn't smoked it.

Wishes he hadn't answered the phone when Jake called.

Wishes his brother hadn't been working a second shift at the plant, *because shit costs money.*

He wishes their father hadn't run off to Atlanta. Or was it Tampa?

He wishes their mom wasn't dead.

But all of these things he wishes hadn't happened did, and so the cogs turn, spooling him into the passenger's seat of this shitty Dodge as Jake pulls off the bypass to get gas.

Jake pumps and Tom Petty plays in the tape deck. It's Friday night, and even over Jake's stereo, Eliot can hear the band on the field, half-time at the stadium, five miles away.

That's why Eliot's surprised to see the dark blue LeBaron, a CHS Swim sticker on the bumper, parked beside an open Dumpster. A stray cat sits on the hood. Watching him. He knows that car, Connie's. *Why isn't she at the game? Fate,* Eliot thinks with a smile.

And inside. Cogs turning. Tape spooling. Recording.

Eliot steps out of the car.

He walks across the Stop-Rite parking lot. Jake's peeled out, Petty blaring. Not really pissed. Not in a permanent way, anyhow.

The Stop-Rite stands in an island of light at the top of a hill on the bypass across from a cornfield. Bats swoop under the pump canopy, eating moths. Georgia in October, and the store windows are fogged, dripping with condensation.

A bell chimes as he opens the front door, and cold air knocks him in the sternum. He glances around, sees no one. Grabs a bag of Funyuns, calculates he can also afford a drink, and mentally rehearses, *Hey, Connie. Hello there. What's a nice girl like you doing in a—no, not that,* as he heads for the machines, passing a Big Slurp on the counter, tall and sweaty. The bent straw tipped pink with lipstick. Next to it, a paperback. Same one he's reading. And now the phone. The receiver off the cradle…

At the far end of the counter, a spinner rack leans akimbo against a stack of Budweiser cases, comic books scattered across the floor. He edges around the stacked beer cases. From behind the counter, he sees, on the floor, a hand, palm up.

He takes another step.

And there: crimped blonde hair, haloed in a pool of red.

He stumbles back, vision blurring, heart racing, blood roaring in his ears even as it spreads beneath her on the floor and he, he has to, he has to get to a phone, he has to help her…

Connie.

CAM 01 / 10/14/94 / 19:20:15:03

A glitch in the tape. Time jump. Six minutes later, out of static and blue October snow, center frame: the counter. An empty space where the girl had been reading. To the left of the frame—("There!")—a boy, kneeling, back to the camera, baggy jeans. Dark hoodie. He stands, turns, stumbling back. A bag of chips in his hands—

("That's the kid, right?"

"That's him. I ran his brother in last year."

"Only a matter of time 'til this one goes to juvie."

The boy looks up at the camera, pupils blown wide, eyes dark, haunted. Guilty?

"We can stop the tape here.")

"I SAID: WHAT WERE YOU DOING HERE?"

The officer stands with his notebook in hand, pen gripped like a gun. Another cop stands behind him, hands on his belt, stance wide.

Eliot can't speak.

He stares down at the Funyuns in his hands, but they aren't his hands anymore.

"Kid? Hey, kid."

There must be proof, Eliot thinks. *Security Cameras.* In that back room, in the glow of the monitors, the security tape. Eliot could play it. Hit PAUSE. On Connie smiling, forever shimmering. Hit REWIND, even, back to the very beginning. To before she ever walked into work that night. Before she ever walked into this job. Then he'd yank out all that black tape, unspool it. So what happened tonight never will, even if it means he, too, will disappear—

But he's already gone. Out on the highway, an eighteen-wheeler roars by, and Eliot feels pulled in its wake, a paper bag waltzing across the bypass, a piece of trash, blown across the asphalt into a cornfield, caught up in the tall, green leaves, the stars wheeling above, there he will be stuck forever waiting for her ghost.

C.O. DAVIDSON'S fiction has appeared on *PseudoPod* and in *Vastarien*, *Cemetery Gates*, and the anthologies *Georgia Gothic* and *Generation X-ed.* She also co-edited *Monsters of Film, Fiction, and Fable*, a collection of scholarly essays. A founding member of the Atlanta Chapter of the Horror Writers Association and a board member for Broadleaf Writers Association, she is a Professor of English at Middle Georgia State University. You can find her on Twitter and Instagram as @colearydavidson.

GONE FISHING
Chris Mann

HE CONVERTED THE STORE from a dilapidated old house he bought for very little money, a bank repo, repaired it with the tender loving care he gave all things wood, all things derivative of nature, and turned it into a place people loved to drop by even if they had no intention of purchasing anything. In the remote reaches of the Ozark Mountain Range of Northern Arkansas, a person couldn't stop just anywhere and get bait, fishing gear, hunting gear, basic hardware, basic groceries, *and* a decent cup of free coffee. The store was retirement money well-spent.

Guy closed up his shop, *Guy's Bait, Tackle, and Hardware*, and put out his favorite sign: "Gone Fishing." He leaned his forehead against the door and took in its smell. He'd used cedar for the door because he loved its smell and softness. He could have used white oak, which is stronger, like he had for the walls, but he thought a door should have a personal touch, be inviting. He'd even glued the cross that the widow Fairstead had given him to the top of the doorframe to help give it a community feel, a sense of sharing, belonging. He hadn't been to church in years, but he still believed in the Almighty.

He took in one last smell of cedar, pulled his head from the door and looked at the trees around him. He had read somewhere that the Ozarks had over 200 species of trees. He liked that thought. The smell of pine was particularly prevalent now in the late spring and the vibrant red and silver the maples produced amazed him every year, and particularly now. He didn't want to leave it. The thought brought emotion into his throat and he reflected upon the phone call.

"I'm sorry, Mr. Anderson, but the tests came back positive," Dr. Minter's nurse had said.

He looked up at the cross above the door and thought about the life he had led. Was it good enough? He snapped his head from side to side and tried to clear his mind.

He reached into his pocket for his keys to lock the door and realized he'd gotten so caught up in his thoughts that he'd forgotten his fishing gear. He went back inside, retrieved it, and locked the door behind him. He would have to tell Thomas about the doctor's report and didn't look forward to that. Thomas, his best friend since high school, had lost his wife to cancer only two years ago.

If a person lives long enough, they will eventually die of cancer. The cells in the body will turn abnormal. They simply cannot regenerate normally for eternity. Someone had told Guy this or he'd read it somewhere, but he couldn't remember who or where. Mostly he couldn't remember because it happened before his diagnosis and because he thought it was the dumbest fucking thing he'd ever heard. A person would die of something at some point and that was just a plain and simple fact. But since first hearing it, he'd thought of how many people old and young died from it. It had been almost a constant thought since the original diagnosis of him having a tumor.

Guy stuffed his slightly overweight 6-foot-3-inch frame into his used, *new to you*, Kia Sportage, another nicety bought with his retirement money, and began the winding drive to meet Thomas at the catfish lake. He looked forward to the fishing but dreaded the conversation.

He sat in the seat with his hand on the key in the ignition and stared straight ahead. He wanted, no, he needed to tell Thomas something else, something much more devastating. Guy knew it might leave him dying in the hospital alone, friendless—he had an affair with Thomas's late wife. It was a mistake nearly 50 years old. It happened right after Vietnam when he had been sent home with a head wound and a Purple Heart, Thomas still serving. It was a shitty thing to do. He hadn't meant to, but that didn't hold water as an excuse. It was a fuck up. Not a mistake. Just a plain fuck up. He'd come so close to telling Thomas about it many times over the years.

"No, that's selfish." He spat it out audibly into the dash of his SUV. "You're going to have to take that one to your grave." He turned the ignition hard with a little bit of anger and a lot of self-loathing.

Guy drove with all the windows down as usual so he could take in the smells—mostly of the blooming flowers, but also the pine—the sounds, a lot of which couldn't be identified as they came raging in as a cacophony of orchestral explosion, and the sights, especially the sights. It was late into the spring and the colors popped from the trees and understory, the layer of vegetation beneath the vastness of tree forest. White oak, short leaf pine, and several species of hickories dominated the trees, but redbuds and dogwoods filled the understory, redbuds adding their brilliant magenta and red dogwoods complementing the redbuds while the white dogwood added striking contrast. Guy figured Heaven had equal, but was sure he'd never see it.

He pulled off the road near the dock of the fairly large catfish lake. Mostly the area had stocked ponds, but everyone in the area considered this one a lake.

"What the heck took you so long?" Thomas said with a big smile. "Thought we were doing our usual time."

"Got held up." He thought of the practiced sympathy of the woman's voice on the phone. "It's not like you ever catch much anyway." Guy gave him his best "fisherman buddy" smile, but today he didn't feel it.

Guy's boat was tied up at the end of the short dock, a privilege the owner of this stocked lake allowed, and Thomas knelt fidgeting with the rope.

"Step aside, old man, and let me get that." Guy grinned as he said it. It was good to see Thomas's always cheerful face.

"Oh, witty. At least I still have my hair." Thomas stood and ran his hand through his hair, almost entirely silver but still thick.

"Bald is beautiful, baby." The banter was as familiar to Guy as the sound of the hop toads along the bank of the lake. He knelt to untie the rope and free the boat from the dock.

Guy had purchased the boat barely used, much like his Kia, and it would be his last major purchase so he could manage his retirement on his fixed income. It was a solid purchase, though, as it was a solid boat—a Sun Dolphin Pro 120, a two-seater. It came with a small Minn Kota trolling motor that served the boat quite well with five forward speeds and three reverse speeds.

He finished untying the boat, but held onto the rope.

"Alright. Get in." Guy still knelt. In his youth, he would have stood back up, but now, now it was easier to simply stay kneeling until it was his turn.

Thomas quickly eased his smaller, wirier frame into the boat. Guy handed Thomas their fishing gear and the cooler of beer Thomas had brought, wrapped the rope one time around the dock cleat, and clumsily rolled into the boat from his knees. He unwrapped the rope from the cleat, cranked up the trolling motor, and headed for the southwest section of the lake. He liked that corner because he liked to fish from the sun casting into the shade. He thought that gave him an advantage.

Once he settled on a spot, Guy opened up the container of punch bait and started to load his hook.

"Man, that stuff smells." Thomas buried his nose into the sleeve of his shirt.

"Yeah, that's why they call it 'stink' bait." Guy put the chunk of bait up to his nose and inhaled deeply as though he had picked a richly scented flower. He offered some to Thomas.

Thomas shook his head no. "I'm going to try something different."

"You know it's mostly channel cats in here."

"Yeah, but there are some blues." Thomas attempted to get a piece of shad and two worms onto his hook at the same time. "And blues like live bait—"

"That chunk of shad is dead," Guy interrupted with a grin.

"That's what the worms are for, make it look alive. Besides the shad is freshly dead, still has its fresh smell."

"See, that's why you never catch anything. Always trying something new."

Thomas looked up from working his hook. "It's not like you're a champion angler."

"Maybe not, but I'm going to continue to play the percentages."

Guy cast his baited hook into the shaded area about 25 feet from the bank. His float bobbed up and down with the ripples of the small waves.

Thomas continued, "How many cats you catch in your last tournament?"

"A couple," Guy said.

"Two. You caught two over the entire length of the tournament. And that was a three-day tournament, right?"

Guy sat down on his chair and reached into the ice chest for a beer. "Want one?"

"Sure." Thomas finished baiting the hook and cast out toward the middle of the lake. One of the worms fell off during the cast. Guy noticed and chuckled.

"Shut up," Thomas said, as he took hold of the Miller Lite, "you have that stupid float bobbing up and down in the water like always. You think they can't see that?"

"Not when I'm fishin' in the shade. I've told you a thousand times, shadows and movements are all they see and ain't smart enough to tell the difference of what kind. Besides, the float tells me when they strike. Gives me an edge."

"Huh-uh, and I listened those 'thousand times.' Seen same results about a thousand times, too," Thomas replied with a tone of amusement in his voice.

Guy noticed the flowers blooming not far from the bank under the shade. Pink begonias mixed with white and green angel wings. God, he loved spring in the Ozarks.

"I got word back from Dr. Minter's office today." Guy took a drink of his beer. "It was from an appointment I had last week."

"I knew something was up," Thomas replied staring straight ahead.

"How's that?" Guy asked trying to act as casual as Thomas.

"You had an appointment a month ago or so. You said you had a new prescription. You cancelled lunch on me twice."

"Cancelled lunch on you?" Guy turned to look at him.

"The way you like to eat, you don't cancel lunch." Thomas continued to face the middle of the lake and took a long pull from his beer. "I figured it was something pretty serious or just something pretty."

"Pretty?"

"Like maybe they hired an older nurse or something."

"I'm not good enough for the young ones?"

"You're not good enough for the old ones either. Never stops you from trying."

"Screw you," Guy replied. He shook his head and smiled.

Thomas chuckled, but without much joy in it. Guy gave a weak grunt and stared at his float. Thomas reeled his line in by around ten feet.

"How serious is it?" Thomas asked.

"Both biopsies came back positive, bladder and prostate." Guy finished his beer in two large gulps, opened the ice chest, put the empty bottle in the ice chest, pulled out another one, opened it, tossed the top into the chest and closed it again.

"That isn't the best news," Thomas said.

"I'll say."

"But those are two of the most curable cancers."

"They want to check for more," Guy said.

"I see."

"Make double sure it's not in the liver or, God help me, the pancreas."

"Yeah. That wouldn't be good."

"What do you think?" Guy asked.

"Did they catch it early?"

"They think they got it early, yeah."

"That's good," Thomas said.

"But I meant, what do you think about it spreading? I mean, should I worry?"

"Being a battlefield medic didn't give me much study in cancer treatment," Thomas said.

"Come on, Thomas, I know you know something about it." Guy stood.

"Okay," Thomas started slowly and took a drink of his beer.

"Just say it."

"The good thing is that the two most often don't have anything to do with each other, meaning that one wouldn't immediately jump to the other."

"That sounds promising," Guy said.

Thomas settled into his chair a little deeper. "If cancer started in the prostate before the bladder, it would most likely go to the bone or lymph system first."

"They're going to do some specific CT scans and specific types of blood work. They want to check the lymph system, the nodes, the pancreas…"

"It sounds like you're going to be okay. I bet they caught it real early," Thomas said.

"And if the bladder cancer was there already? I mean, could it have gone to the prostate?"

Thomas's line went taut and he jerked the rod.

"I think I got him," Thomas said in an excited high-pitched tone.

"Shit, yeah! You got him!"

Thomas worked the reel pretty hard for three turns and then held the line taut. He pulled it a little, reeled a little, and let it stay taut again. He worked the fish in this manner until he had it close to the boat. Guy watched Thomas work the fish and then grabbed the net.

"Bring him a little closer," Guy instructed.

Thomas gave the rod one continuous smooth pull over his shoulder.

"There! I got him." Guy pulled the fish into the boat and cautiously removed the hook from its mouth. He held up the fish. "Damn, Thomas, that is one pretty hefty blue."

"Yes, it is!" Thomas stood to admire his work close up. "What do you think? 25, 30 pounder?"

"More like 35, maybe even 40. He's pretty damn heavy." Guy put the fish into the basket and dropped the basket, which was tied to the boat cleat, into the water. He didn't like using stringers because they might get away. That and he would have to pierce the fish again and more solidly. He didn't like causing them any more pain than he had to.

"Alright. That's one fish." Thomas held his Miller Lite up and they clinked bottles and took a swallow.

Guy sat down again and grabbed his fishing rod. He had gotten so caught up in Thomas's catch that he totally forgot about his gear. Good thing a fish hadn't struck his line yet, he thought. It was a damn expensive reel and one he'd planned on leaving to Thomas.

Thomas cleared his throat. "Guy, these are a couple of the most curable cancers around. You should be good."

Guy stared at his float bobbing up and down with the small waves. "I'm scared."

"That's understandable."

"Not of dying." Guy's head suddenly filled with thoughts of wasted opportunities and regretful moments. One, 50-year-old deed in particular, dangled like a meat hook in his mind.

"What are you scared of then, the bill?" Thomas asked and grabbed another beer.

"I'm scared of going to hell," Guy said.

"For the love of God, why?" Thomas turned to face him.

"Wouldn't you be afraid of hell?" Guy's voice raised slightly with agitation.

"You're not going to hell." Thomas's voice was calm and even.

"I haven't lived a good enough life."

"You've done plenty of good."

"I'm selfish, hard-headed, cranky…" Guy didn't want to continue going, but it felt like a flood coming out.

"Anyone wants something from your store and you don't have it, you order it and then you keep stocking it. Even if it costs you money. You always try and help people, make them feel good. This is your boat and you treat it like it's ours. Hell, you don't even put the fish on a stringer. You had to buy that expensive box," Thomas said.

Thomas looked at Guy for a minute and Guy could feel Thomas's eyes taking something in, sizing him up.

"What? You don't think people notice?" You're a great guy, Guy." Thomas snorted gently, friendly.

"You're right I always help."

"See," Thomas said.

"I help myself to whatever the fuck I want."

"Huh?" Thomas looked genuinely confused.

"The beer, the fishing—"

"I like fishing." Thomas looked Guy in the eyes, squinting slightly. "I like beer."

"But it's not your favorite kind! It's my favorite kind!" Guy stood up.

"So, what?"

"That's selfish of me!"

"What the hell are you talking about?" Thomas asked.

Guy looked down as if the lake might open up and swallow him. He saw the cross on the door of his shop, heard the voice on the phone, thought of Thomas's wife. All of the sudden, the beauty of nature--the sweet smells, calming sounds, and glorious colors--turned into a choking combination of punch bait odor, endless white noise of bugs and toads, and a rich, deep red of guilt.

"I slept with Diana." The words burned Guy's throat as if he threw up pure bile.

"My wife? You're talking about my Diana?" Thomas asked.

"Yeah. Why the hell would I tell you about some other Diana?"

"I don't know. You're kind of bouncing all over the place. Topic wise, I mean."

"Yes, Thomas, your fucking wife…sorry, I mean your sweet lady, wonderful woman. God! All of that sounds bad, crazy."

Thomas looked out across the lake. He inhaled a deep breath with his mouth and slowly released it through his nose.

"I knew, I mean, I know," Thomas said calmly.

"Damn right! Terrible human being!"

"Calm down."

"Ah, fuck! I shouldn't have said anything. What the fuck am I doing?"

"No. Listen to me. Stop freaking out." Thomas motioned for Guy to sit down. He waited for Guy to sit. He allowed Guy to take a couple of breaths and took a couple for himself before continuing. "I knew about that a long time ago."

"What?" Guy's shock caused him to feel numb, weak. It's a good thing he had sat down.

"Right after you got discharged from the service, she took good care of you."

"Yeah," Guy said confused.

"She wrote me and told me what happened." Thomas turned his reel a few times bringing the hook in a little closer.

"I don't understand you." Guy felt his guts start to turn a little and his face felt flush.

"Wounded soldier, Purple Heart, a hero comes home. Be thankful someone appreciated that. A lot of people didn't."

"You saying she had sex with me and that's how she appreciated me? What about you still being over there? What about that fucking appreciation?" Guy practically screamed it and it echoed off the mountains.

Thomas stood and grabbed Guy hard around his right bicep and Guy felt Thomas's strong hands digging into his arm. Underneath them the boat swayed erratically.

"Hey, I don't blame Diana, okay. Don't ever say that I should. Don't ever say something like that to me again. Lonely, not knowing if I'd come back. All that shit with people protesting, not supporting us. Diana was a sweet woman. I don't blame her. She was honest. She wrote me and told me. That was that. Hell, I thought you knew I knew. That's why I never mentioned it."

Thomas released Guy's arm. Guy fidgeted with his reel as he tried to soak in what he'd just heard.

"Look at me." Thomas's voice possessed a definitive sternness now, almost military in its command.

"What?"

"Look me in the eyes," Thomas demanded.

Guy turned to Thomas and looked him squarely in the eyes. It was easy to see how this little wiry guy had come out of Vietnam alive and with a full tour as a medic. Thomas's jaw was set, firm, and a different look had sprung into his eyes.

"I did not hate you," Thomas started and paused only slightly for effect. "Never did. Never have. Never will."

"Goddamn it, Thomas," Guy started to turn, but Thomas grabbed him by the shoulder and spun him in order to maintain eye contact. Once again, the boat rocked in complaint.

"I wasn't ready to rush up and give you a giant hug and be blood brothers, but I never hated you." Thomas was firm, unwavering, but still seemed somehow positive. Guy always liked that about him. Thomas was the kind of person that you just couldn't hate. The kind of person Guy had always wanted to be.

"That's fucked up," Guy said quietly. It was almost a whisper, almost as though he was talking to himself.

"Look, this is how I figured it. You listening?"

"Yeah. I'm listening."

"I mean really listening because I don't ever want to talk about this again," Thomas said.

Guy nodded. Thomas sat down and motioned for Guy to do the same. Thomas took a sip of his beer and a deep breath before he started.

"The way I figured it, she either loved you and that was that or she didn't and we'd get married and move on."

"Christ, that's crazy," Guy said, his voice distant.

"But she did love you, Guy, she just wasn't *in* love with you. There's a big difference. So, we moved on. That's why we took the long vacation, just the two of us. Remember?"

"Yeah, that was odd."

"No kidding. How many people came back from a tour in 'Nam and then left home again in order to get away?" Thomas asked.

"Nobody. Everyone was clingin' to every family member they had, every piece of home they missed." Guy could see his family waiting at the front door for him like it happened yesterday.

"Exactly. Mom was ticked at me for leaving the same week I got back."

"No, she was fuckin' pissed."

"Yes, she was. But Diana and I had to get away. Get some room for us and just us. See what we still had and didn't have," Thomas said.

"So, you weren't pissed at me?" Guy asked.

"A little, but weren't we all pissed about something when we got back? Or at nothing? Or at everything?"

Guy let the conversation sit for a minute. He opened the cooler and feigned looking into it. He closed it again.

"I'm sorry," Guy said.

"I know."

"And I'm sorry for—"

"Confession is good for the soul," Thomas interrupted. "And I'm here for you anyway I can. But, from now on, let's leave my wife out of it."

"Yeah. No problem."

"Good."

Thomas opened up a package of potato chips. "Now let's catch some more fish," he said through a mouthful of chips. "We gotta have at least one more so we have enough to eat."

Guy opened his eyes wide and took in a deep breath as though waking from a nap. He began reeling in his line. "Let me try a little bit of that shad that you brought, this punch bait ain't workin'."

"Alright." Thomas handed over the container of bait fish and the can of worms.

"Thanks," Guy said. "Alright, two worms and one piece of shad, right?"

"Yeah, but put the shad on first and then the two worms," Thomas said.

"Okay."

Guy worked on getting the hook baited. Thomas reeled in his line.

"I think I'm going to try and cast in the shade. See what kind of luck I have," Thomas said.

Guy looked up at the western sky. "Going to be a lot of shade here in a minute."

"We should catch more than one fish then. Lot of 'em like to feed at dusk."

"I hear that." Guy finished baiting his hook. "Think I'll cast this one out toward the middle. Try my luck there."

Guy stood up, reared back and cast the line as far out as he could, reeled it in a couple of turns, and sat back down in his seat. His mind drifted to Thomas's forgiveness, mainly his capacity for it. Surely, the Almighty had capacity for it, too, an even greater amount of it. It was a thought Guy planned to cling to. He finally felt good, clean.

Facing the middle of the lake, he could smell the witch hazels as they lined the bank on the opposite side. They were plentiful and their pale yellow and reddish-purple colors stood out underneath the black walnut trees that also lined the bank a little farther from the water. In the distance, he heard the echo of a Whippoorwill signaling the setting of the sun.

CHRIS MANN is a multi-award-winning playwright and stage director. He is two-time winner of a Kennedy Center/ACTF Award for Outstanding New Play (*Dancing in the Afternoon, Smells Like Rain*). His plays have been produced in such venues as EST/LA, The Asylum, Chicago Dramatists, Flatiron Playhouse (NYC), and The French Institute in Edinburgh, Scotland. He has published numerous short stories in literary magazines such as *The Rio Grande Review* and *Sellouts*. Mann also enjoys writing speculative fiction. His most recent story, "One Way or Another," can be found in the anthology *Road Kill: Texas Horror* by Texas Writers, vol. 6. from Death's Head Press.

Somewhere Anywhere

Kevin Brown
Previously Appeared in *Night Terrors Anthology*, 2010

5:45 A.M.

Skylar Mosely gunned the throttle on his old man's fishing boat and the nose lifted high off the dark water, the current splitting white around the aluminum body. Squinting, he snaked around the bends of the river, watching the dark treetops limned ahead. His earlobes were red and stinging. His eyes watered in the cold push of air.

An hour ago, he'd snuck out dressed in layers of hunting clothes and hitched the boat to the pick-up. It was his dad's truck and boat, and Skylar wasn't allowed to take them out alone. But he'd decided to after his dad came home tanked and smelling not like his mom's perfume. They'd yelled and cried and slammed things until he passed out, and she went to the Motor Inn Motel. This had been happening more and more, and Skylar figured that if they could have their places to go, so could he.

Skylar watched the snow-splotched banks slide by. Felt the foamy spray of water on the backs of his hands like ice needles. He bit down hard, and his jaw squared off and popped. He was sick of the liquor and women, the fighting and cruelty. Lately, he wondered what was going on in his old man's mind when he slammed tools in the garage. When he stabbed food on his plate as if it were alive, shoveling it in his mouth faster than he could chew and swallow. Always looking down or to the side, answering questions in grunts or nods. He wondered where that anger had come from and how far it was going to go.

Skylar eased off the throttle and angled the boat toward a fallen cedar near the bank. His dad had never taken him upriver this far, and the land felt foreign and undiscovered. He'd heard game ran wild in this area because few people hunted it—if you were lucky enough to bag a good-sized deer, getting it back would be a chore, and most folks didn't bother. But he figured he'd cross that bridge when and if he came to it.

He'd also heard stories of these woods being haunted. It was where that family, the Otis's, had supposedly lived. Where, if you believed the tales, they were murdered—burned alive, one at a time. Son and daughter first. And according to the older folks in town, where the house stands to this day, the four charred spots are still burned into the floorboards.

Skylar stepped onto the muddy bank bottom and tied the boat off. Shouldered his .30-06 and looked around, his breath ghosting out white. Currents rolled and flecked in the river, but everything else was a numb silence. He climbed the bank by the jutting tree roots and stepped into the woods, sinking calf-high in the snow. He felt oddly comfortable, as if the land were closing its arms around him. Pulling him in a hug to its breast.

6:40 A.M.

Nature began to form and take shape with the light. The world one large Polaroid being shaken until it developed. The brush came alive, rattling. Twigs snapped. Parts of dead trees cracked off and popped the snow. It seemed the lighter it got, the louder. And colder.

Skylar sat on a dark tree root that crooked out of the snow like a burned elbow. The wind seemed to come from all directions, chipping away at his face and neck. A few feathering snowflakes had turned into a sideways flurry, and it was hard to see more than thirty yards out. The snow's surface was smooth as white cake icing.

He flipped his collar up and slid his hands under his armpits, balancing the rifle in his lap. He imagined his mom shifting and tossing under worn motel sheets. Her face clenched in the middle, eyes red and raw. And his dad, still sprawled sideways on the bed, half-dressed and snoring. He couldn't understand why his father continued to stray off the straight, simple road he and Skylar's mom had been on for twenty-one years, or why he took highways and side roads headed in every direction but home.

He thought about their vacation a year ago. It was the last great time he could remember them having together. They'd gone to Clearwater, Florida, and every day they ate at a different seafood restaurant. He and his dad played Frisbee on the beach. They tossed hunks of bread in the air for the screeching seagulls to dive and catch, and watched the sun deflate into the horizon, where it watered off and on to somewhere, anywhere.

In beach chairs behind him, his mom and dad sipped margaritas and laughed and kissed, while Skylar sat in the surf, curling his toes in the warm wet sand, the water foaming in and over and around him, then sliding metallic back into the sea.

He shifted on the root, looked out ahead, and thought about that old house and if it was really out here somewhere, all decayed and folding in on itself, animal tracks and wads of shit everywhere. He wondered what direction it was supposed to be in and if he was close.

The way he'd heard it, the Otis's lived back here in the 1930s. People called them river rats because they lived on what they took from the river. Some claimed to have seen them occasionally, running trotlines and barrel nets for fish and turtles. They were supposed to be inbred and ravaged by syphilis. Disfigured by chancres and patchy hair, pegged and notched screwdriver teeth. Brain disorders.

Story goes, they took in a couple of guys lost in the woods one night. What they didn't know was these guys had robbed and killed a goods store owner twenty miles north and took to the woods. They fed them, gave them a change of clothes, and a bed for the night.

And sometime the next morning…

Skylar looked around, scanning the thickets and bottoms. He wondered if years ago, killers had actually come through this exact area, maybe rested on this same elbow root. If they saw chimney smoke mouse-tailing above the trees. Faint candlelight in the windows like eyes. He wondered if all those years ago, you could smell burnt flesh in the air. Blood and charred hair in the leaves. He figured not, because he'd also heard the Otis's weren't fried like witches, they'd just moved on, farther upriver where the fish were more abundant. Lived and died the way most people lived and died. Uneventfully.

Some swear they never even existed.

To his left, there was a loud crack in the underbrush, and he jerked around. Leaned forward and raised his rifle. Another snap and he saw it—a jackrabbit working its nose in the air, ears twitching. It spun and sputtered into the tangle, and Skylar eased his gun back across his lap, wiping his nose with the back of his hand. He glanced to his right and nearly fell backward, off the root.

Standing there, forty yards out and staring at him, was a large, wide-racked buck.

It'd never made a sound, just appearing out of nowhere like a ghost.

6:45 A.M.

Skylar whipped his gun up as the buck turned to bolt. He squinted, threaded the bead on its shoulder, and fired.

6:46 A.M.

Blood was everywhere. Standing where the deer had been, breathing heavy, he could still hear it bouncing through the thicket ahead. He wasn't sure where he hit him, but it was deep enough. Thick ropes of blood trailed off from where he stood, toward the sounds the deer was making.

Skylar ate a handful of snow, pinched his collar, and fanned his shirt. He looked back in the direction he'd come from, toward the river. Large foot divots sat in the snow like candle holes in cake frosting.

He turned back toward the unseen world snapping and popping and dying ahead. He started after it.

8:15 A.M.

Skylar leaned over, hands on his knees, trying to catch his breath. His lungs felt scrubbed raw inside and he coughed and spat. He'd come a ways, the deep snow hampering his movements. Several times he thought he'd lost the trail and was about to turn back, when a slash of red on a tree or a glob in the snow pulled him along. He'd been through a rotten cane patch woven with vines of briers, and farther, until looking back, the black oaks and cedar trees looked like walls. Like jaws closing out the open world forever.

Still coughing, Skylar yelled, "Better be one big fucking deer!" and his voice sounded small.

He kept going—up the incline of a ridge, along its spine. Down the slope, the snow sliding around him, and—

Before he heard it, he almost ran right into it. He dropped to his knees, slipped his coat off, and clutched a tree trunk. Leaning forward, he drank handfuls of icy stream water that swirled by, dark as the trees, then disappeared around the bend.

8:23 A.M.

Skylar wiped his mouth on his shirtsleeve and looked around. The trail picked up on the other side of the stream, and unless there was a narrower spot to cross, that was it. Curtain call. He was done.

He leaned back down for another drink, and the small bank loosened and caved. He whimpered and slipped face forward toward the water. Never breaking grip with the tree, his body spun, and his legs went in instead.

He sunk gut deep, his feet hitting the bottom.

As quickly as he went in, he grabbed the tree with his other hand and pulled himself out. The water had taken his breath, and his clothes were slick and shiny and clinging to his body as if they were melting.

AN HOUR LATER.

Skylar's hands fluttered. His jaw quivered. He'd started back, following his own ghost of a trail, as the older tracks were disappearing, erased by the storm. He'd slid his coat on and jammed his hands under his armpits, carrying the rifle in his folded arms. But the shaking had intensified. His toes seemed to have disappeared a while back, and his pants were stiffening and freezing to his legs. He fell several times, and each fall he seemed to leave a little more of his energy, of himself, in the snow.

He reached the cane patch and made his way in. He scanned the ground, the tracks barely imprinted on the surface. He went left, lost the trail. Turned back and followed the tracks he'd just made. The briers bit into his clothes, tore at his cheeks and ears. Cane sprung at his face, popping him in the forehead. He stumbled and regained balance, turned and went in any direction, clawing, trying to find some landmark that looked familiar. "Please," he said, and saw an opening ahead. He went toward it in a rush, the thorns ripping into him, and finally made it out of the tangle. He stopped. Dropped to his knees.

There was the stream, the bank caved in by the tree.

He looked around. Every thicket and stunted cedar, log and bush looked the same, like black and white Xeroxed copies in all directions. He tried to stand and dropped his rifle. Tripped and sunk. He slammed his fist into the ice and screamed, but it muffled in the flurry. The wind moaned around him. For some reason, he pictured his mom on the nights she waited up for his dad, her eyes rimmed in tears. Imagined the *tack, tack, tacking* of her wedding ring on the tabletop.

And for the first time, he began to think he might die. He started to wonder if his death would somehow reunite his parents, maybe make them see what real unhappiness is. Through his tragedy, their marriage would live on. A sacrifice of him for the better them.

He smiled and began to cry.

LATER.

Skylar nestled between two oak logs, draped his coat over his legs, and closed his eyes. His hands trembled in a violent blur and his lips had gone the color of veins under the skin. His eyelids were bruise-purple and as translucent as a baby bird's. He tried to listen for a passing boat, some sign that would show him the direction the river was in. Back to where his dad's boat was roped off and waiting to take him somewhere warm. To his family. His home. He was about to nod off when he heard a child's voice giggle and say, "You dead?"

He opened his eyes.

In front of him, a little girl was wrapped in a dirty brown coat, wearing yellow socks as mittens.

He started to cry again.

"You *ain't* dead!" she said. Tears slid off his cheeks and he shook his head "no."

She reached out and wrapped both hands around one of his, grunted, and tugged. He winced, snakes of pain coiling through his legs. She tugged harder and said, "Come *on*, silly." He shifted, and the cold around his joints seemed to crack and release. He staggered to his feet, a lapful of snow dusting down.

She turned to go, still holding one of his hands, but he didn't move. "Well?" she said. "You coming or ain't ya?"

He took a step and fell. She helped him up and he took another, then another, his movements jerky and stilted. He stared at the back of her head, her dirty blonde curls floating in the wind. In a breathless fragment, he said, "Where...we going?"

Not looking back, she giggled.

"Hey..." he said, "do you...know?"

"Course I do, *silly*," she said, and giggled again. She stopped and pointed down the hill at a small, earthy looking house. "Home."

She yanked his hand and he fell again. They staggered down the hill.

The house looked like it had been twisted in opposite directions from the center like a half-turned Rubik's Cube. A maple had grown through the back porch and bent over the roof. Smoke spiraled from the chimney, which was crumbling and leaning in the opposite direction of the house. The windows were glazed in a caul of ice and a shutter creaked back and forth on its hinges like and oscillating fan.

They went in.

The front door was crooked, and the house shifted and bowed under his footsteps. The walls were decayed and peeling like skin. In the beams of light filtered through the tattered curtains, he saw rats crisscross on the countertops. Something dark slipped across his boot and disappeared in the shadows with liquid grace.

The little girl began to hum "This Little Light of Mine." She skipped ahead, into the living room, and said, "In here, reindeer."

"Where's your...mom and dad?" Skylar said. He jerked forward.

Backlit by the fire in the hearth, she giggled and sang: *"Let it shine, let it shine, le-et it shine!"*

The wind gripped the house and shook it. The shutter slammed against the sill. He jumped and looked around.

"You can sit down," she said, and he heard her moving around in the dark. He eased into a dusty chair that wobbled under his weight. She poured something and appeared out of the shadows with a coffee mug. He watched her face—her dirt-smudged cheeks and runny nose. Her missing front tooth.

She handed him the mug. "Cocoa," she said, and winked. Still humming, she slipped a moldy gray blanket around his shoulders. She stepped back into the dark.

"Your...parents?" he said again, his words cutting out. He cupped the mug in both hands. Felt the heat in his palms. He took a drink and his chest warmed.

"You ought not wander around out there by yourself," she said. "There's bears, ya know?"

He took a drink, never taking his eyes off her. The house shook again and popped. The shutter slammed. He pulled the blanket tight and held it under his chin. "What's your name?" he said, his voice stronger.

And she said, "Wanna hear a story?" She stoked the logs in the fire, and it lit up the room. And then he saw it.

Four charred spots in the floor, burned straight through the boards to the ground.

His throat went dry. Skin needled and detached from everything it held inside.

"One a ponce of the time," she said, giggling, "there was a beautiful princess—"

"This is the Otis house, ain't it?" he said, unable to take his eyes from the floor. "It's really real."

"—and one day the princess was captured by a mean ol' dragon and locked in a fiery dungeon—"

"How…?" he said, and his voice was weak again.

She stepped out of the shadows, still smiling, and said, "—one day, a handsome prince arrived at the dragon's den to rescue the princess…" and a fleshy bubble pulsed and formed under her right eye and wormed down her face. Dropped in a hot pucker mark on the floor. Her hair singed at the ends of her curls, hissed, and began to blacken in spirals to her scalp. More bubbles rose, shiny in the light, and slid off and onto the floor.

He tried to move but was frozen.

Her lips peeled back in a gap-toothed grimace. Steam wavered around her.

"…and he told the dragon: 'Release the princess, dragon, or face the blade of my sword!'"

He swallowed, starting to shiver. "You're…dead," he said, barely a whisper.

She stopped talking. Then, her voice dragging slower and slower like a damaged audiotape, said, "I'm not dead, *silly*," and disappeared.

His breath caught. He looked down and his hands were cupped, holding nothing. He looked back up and there was no house. No darkened living room or fire in the hearth. No charred floor. Only snow and thickets and trees that all looked the same.

Sitting on the ground, half-covered from the blizzard, there was not even a moldy blanket draped around him.

SOMETIME. ANYTIME.

Skylar huddled against a large oak, between its flanges that opened out into thick roots. Eyes closed. Face pale and puffy. From somewhere far away he heard the faint growl of a boat motor on the river, but he didn't open his eyes. He'd just sit awhile and wait. Stay here and rest a little longer because he knew sometimes boats weren't boats at all. Sometimes, you heard boats like you saw old houses and little girls humming in the woods. He'd just stay here and relax, listen to the seagulls screech in the warmth of the sun. Smile at his mom and dad sitting in beach chairs behind him, laughing and sipping margaritas. Together and happy. Maybe he and his dad would toss the Frisbee along the beach. So what if that was a boat, there'd be more. There was always more. There were boats and boats, and he could sail away anytime. Toward the sun deflating into the horizon, where it watered off to somewhere, anywhere. But now, he just wanted to sit in the surf and curl his toes in the warm wet sand. Listen to the waves hiss and burst. Let the salty water foam in and over and around him, then slip silver back into the sea.

Really, it could wait.

He was warm now.

Even the shivering had stopped.

KEVIN BROWN has published two short story collections, *Death Roll* and *Ink On Wood*, and has had fiction, non-fiction and poetry published in over 200 literary journals, magazines and anthologies. He won numerous writing competitions, fellowships, and grants, and was nominated for multiple prizes and awards, including three Pushcart Prizes.

DEVIL'S FOOTPRINT ON MY CHIN:
THE GREAT AWAKENING OF IRIS BLUE LUCKADOO BIVENS
Mary Alice Dixon

> *"…my subject in fiction is the action of grace in territory*
> *largely held by the devil."*
>
> —Flannery O'Connor

MADE ME MAD AS ALL HELLFIRE seeing the burying ground Good Shepherd been blinded. Both eyes gone. Cored out like rotten apples. Nose hacked off, too. Even his fat little sheep fleeced of their heads, sliced with clean cuts nature don't make but your cordless Black & Decker sure does. What damn fool hits up a 10-foot oak statue of Christ Jesus standing smack top of the only hill in Hope Springs Eternal Gardens? Shepherd's been rising there long as I remember, above a patchwork quilt of slate headstones lying in pea-green crabgrass and dirty yellow straw. Now my first day on the job, he's mutilated.

I knew who Hope Gospel Church folks were gonna blame. Me. They'd say see how evil follows Iris Blue. Church faithful believed my granny's testifying that I bore the devil's footprint in the grape-stain dimple on my chin.

"Girl's damned," the pastor had said, and me just a young'un. Hosanna'ed over me a hundred times in a voice of exclamation points but could not pray the purple off my face.

Granny Blue came clear from West Virginia to raise me when my mama died, came from the hollers where old women see signs in skies and sin in skin. But here in Hope Springs, North Carolina, where red clay runs flat from Charlotte, people ought know better. Ought know a big-bodied gal such as myself is good for graveyard grounds keeping, growing up, as I did, in my daddy's landscaping business. Working dirt.

Though church folk called that wicked, too. Said was no business for a girl hoping for a husband and salvation. But I never aimed to be a house-locked or a church-chained woman.

When Pastor's exorcisms failed, Granny sought to remove the stain upon me, wanted me to pass without signing what I was. She soaked scrub rags in comfrey and sour lemon piss, bound them tight around my chin. Didn't work. Turned my dimple scaly sapphire blue like a bruise that never healed.

Daddy, he just said, "Don't give it no mind, Iris Blue, beauty mark is what you got."

Granny hated Daddy, contended Mama married down. Granny ran Daddy off when he planted the honeycrisp tree out front. Granny said Daddy knew she hated apples. Granny had a lot of hates, hated Daddy's whole long Luckadoo line. Would have hated Buck Bivens, too, but she died before I met him.

Buck Bivens, he's my husband, though way he treats me, thinks he's my boss man. Blew up at me this morning about my Walmart Weed B-Gone.

"Weed killer you're pouring round the tomatoes gonna do us in. Roots suck it right up. Use your pea brain, just once do something right."

Sprawled on his butt in the turquoise yard chair by our old woodshed, bottle of Skeeters Cherry Bourbon in his hand. At 10 a.m. on a Monday morning. Were Granny living yet, she'd say church bells gonna sweat blood fearing for Buck's almighty soul. Me? I say, he can go to hell.

"You're lookin' mighty pissed there, girl. Relax, smell the roses."

"I ain't no girl, we ain't got no roses, and you don't know nothing about weed killing."

"When's that job interview you got at the graveyard?"

"Told you a thousand times, noon."

"I'll take lunch now since you're fixing to head off."

Buck was my mistake. Met him two years back after my last girlfriend dumped me. I was living lonely, feeling fat, going broke, and figured what the hell, I've always played for both teams, so let's try me a man again. Buck wooed me by claiming he was gonna make it big in some scheme his fancy Atlanta art gallery gal called "outsider art." Like I said, my mistake.

"I'm an artist, darlin'," he'd said, sitting tall in the orange tufted-back booth I worked at Fat Boys Pancakes off Independence Boulevard up to Charlotte. Lifted his aviator shades, gave me the once over.

"But I'd need to be Mr. *Michael Angelo* himself to sculpt your fulsome curves. Always did like me a ginger-haired gal with meat on her bones. And the devil in her face."

Buck gave me a tip. I gave him my number. Ten years older than me, but too young at 51 to be lookin' to me as a nurse and a purse, though that's what he got. Me, all I got was made and unsatisfactorily laid.

Gallery gal from Atlanta disappeared real fast after Buck and me married. I reckon the so-called market for that outsider art disappeared, too. I been supporting us both working Fat Boys 'til it closed last month, right before Memorial Day.

Artist, my ass. Man spends nights out partying, days drinking in the shed, carving garden trolls from junk wood he calls "found objects." Ugly as sin. Evil-eyed critters with big bellies and pointy heads. Tries to sell 'em at the Monroe Sweet Union Flea Market on weekends when he's not too drunk to drive.

"Stop your lollygagging, get me lunch."

Buck, still hung over from whatever bar he haunted last night, took another swig of Skeeters, pulled his floppy straw Tommy Bahama knockoff hat over his face. He was probably gallivanting about with that bottle-blonde hussy Earlene Singer, one who runs Velvet Hand nail salon beside Fat Boys. One of her Tangerine Tiger acrylic fingernails turned up in our bathtub last week. Hers, alright, judging by the gold glitter glued to its tip.

Dwelling on Buck and Earlene fired me up. I marched through the rickety paint-peeling back door into what Granny used to call our shotgun house, "shot right out of hell," she'd say, turning her nose up at the yellow vinyl siding bearing black mold and green mildew. House suited me just fine, though that damned shed holding Buck's trolls was a nasty spot smelling of rotten wood.

"Chow time, *Michael Angelo*," I yelled out the door, after slapping slices of sweet tomato and bitter honeycrisp on Wonder Bread, heavy on the Duke's mayo.

Buck hoisted himself up and tripped over one of his hunchback trolls in the crabgrass.

"You're tipsy, eat you some of this, you'll get to feeling better." I handed him the sandwich on one of Granny's mustard-brown melamine plates. "Picked your lunch up at the Food Lion last night." I felt no guilt in lying.

Twenty minutes later Buck keeled over. Face down on the kitchen floor. "Buck, you alive?"

He rolled over, choking. "Go, get away from me, she-devil." Then he passed out.

I considered calling 9-1-1 but didn't. I threw on blue denim overalls, rubbed Maybelline peach concealer on my chin, and left Buck lying on the linoleum.

AT HOPE SPRINGS ETERNAL GARDENS I waited for my job interview in a windowless brick reception hall. Brocade curtains concealed body viewing rooms. Thick air smelled of formaldehyde and stale lilies. Caskets for sale lined up like a funeral procession awaiting mourners. Far as I could tell, one of those babies would set a body back a decade of Chevy payments, minimum.

I stood quiet, studying on a white-haired woman sitting slumped in the manager's corner cubicle. She cleared her throat, hearing aid making a high-pitched whine. "About the money, Mister C, thing is, gotta wait on the social security check."

"No worries," a deep baritone said. "Got a real sweet oak coffin here for your boy, the fellow paid to use it died at sea. Yours, on the house."

Sweet Jesus. I knew that voice. Pelican Crowdermilk. Always the Good Samaritan. Kid who used to put his lunch money in the church poor box.

Pel came out of the office to where I could see him. Looked firm-muscled for a man with a desk job, fat fair face as round and innocent as the first time we kissed back of the gym, seventh grade. Boy was baptized Donnie Lee, but kids called him Pelican, Pel for short, due to how silver-white his hair was and how he picked his ivory skin 'til it was raw. He didn't seem to mind the name. "Pel's your pal, Iris Blue," he'd say to me.

Kids mocked me, too. All but Pel, he stuck up for me. Even the time when Earlene Singer put Elmer's Glue in my locker room shampoo, or when seventh grade boys chased me out of the cafeteria. "Do me, devil's daughter," they yelled, fingering their chins.

"I see the pretty in her," Pel shouted back.

But they just laughed at him.

Pel tried to soften my hurts. He'd draw blue and purple angel faces on index cards he pinched from teacher's table. Wrote my name on each in lilac Sharpie. Called them holy cards. Slipped me one each time we kissed. I grew quite a collection. 'Til we got caught. Pel sought the blame, but teacher whipped me. Called Pel a simple soul. Me, she called a sinner.

"You're looking good, Mrs. Bivens."

"Call me Iris."

"Still pretty as a flower, Iris. Know what this here job involves?"

"I grew up working dirt with my daddy. You remember Luckadoo Landscaping? Apple doesn't fall far from the tree." I laughed. Pel didn't.

"Weed killing, grass mowing, tree planting, I'm built to do it all."

"You'd be the first woman to captain our ground crew."

"I'm my daddy's daughter."

Pel shook my hand, "No, you're not, you're better than him. Start now if you want."

"Okay, boys," I said to the crew by the cinderblock equipment garage. "Name's Iris Blue Luckadoo Bivens. Don't mess with me, I got the sign of Satan on my face." I hooted like it were a joke but not a man smiled.

"I see five of you fellas, two John Deere Z365R lawn mowers, and one Caterpillar hydraulic backhoe. Anything I'm missing?"

They stared at me, quiet as church mice.

"Let's walk, see what needs doing."

"Grave needs dug side of Shepherd hill, boss lady. This way."

"What the hell?" That's when I saw the Good Shepherd's eyes missing, nose gone, his sheep, headless.

"Weren't nothing wrong with Jesus yesterday," one guy said.

"Who wants a sharp-snouted lamb's head? College frat boys?"

"Happened over night, ma'am. Cuts real carpenter-like."

When I pulled up to the house after quitting time first thing I saw was Earlene Singer perched on my front porch glider, all dolled up, pecan pie in her lap.

"Nobody answered the door. Buck gone?"

"Guess so."

"Just wanted to say hey."

"I'll take your pie."

"That's okay, I'll carry it to church circle in the morning." She sashayed down to her Buick, calling over her shoulder. "Pastor says you're killing off the cemetery's Good Shepherd. Bad news travels fast, honey."

Inside I found Buck truly was gone, just not the way I expected. His note said, "Leaving for good." I guess Weed B-Gone don't always work how you think it will.

GOT TO THE GRAVEYARD EARLY the next day, sunrise painting the grass blood red.

"Morning, Iris Blue." Pel bounded out of the office, handed me a thermos of coffee.

"Who's doing this?" I pointed past pink plastic peonies to the Shepherd, now lacking his ears. "I hear tell Pastor's already blaming me. You call the law?"

"No need. I'll make sure Pastor knows you had nothing to do with it."

"You're a godly man, Pel."

"Saw Buck real late last night. With Earlene in the Food Lion. Had a couple of those wooden garden trolls of his in a knapsack."

"Buck?"

"Yelling how some Food Lion sandwich about near killed him, gave him food poisoning. Manager asked them to leave."

I pondered Buck, Shepherd body parts, and the sweet revenge of clearing my name but all I said to Pel was, "Best be getting to my mowing."

Saturday morning I was at Sweet Union Flea Market, hell-bent to catch him. Walked past woven grass baskets, bushels of Gaffney peaches, boxes of broken-looking CB radios. Behind the Bad Dogs & Hot Buns food truck I saw a sunburned gal in cut-offs carrying a wooden nose.

"Where'd you get that?"

"My boy broke his nose, doc said never grow straight, got this here from Hope of Hope Springs. Booth over yonder by the crochet bedspreads. Fella says it's a healing nose."

How much was that bastard charging?

"Blessed ear helps with the earache," a deep baritone said.

Sweet Jesus. Pelican Crowdermilk.

"Let me touch it," said a guy in a gray Concord Mills cap.

"Pel, what the devil?"

"Nice to see you, too, Iris." He smiled, his eyes pure opal in the sun.

"Doing the Lord's work. Hope is a priceless thing."

"Why?"

"Cemetery investors gonna tear down the Shepherd, replace him with a concrete war memorial, saying Shepherd brings too many termites to the trees and too much religion to the burying grounds; they don't want neither. They're not telling the public, wanting to avoid a Church fight. I'm just saving what I can."

"Preying on people. You, of all men."

Concord Mills cap interrupted. "How much for your ear?"

"No charge ever for relics of hope. Yours for the asking, friend."

"Look here, Iris, at this eye. Shepherd's eye awakens sight inside a soul." He put a wooden eye into my palm. "I always did see the pretty in you."

Pel was right about one thing but it weren't the pretty in me. He was right about the Shepherd's eye. It awakened something in me I could not put to sleep. I gave the eye back to Pel.

"Come on over to the house round sunset. I'll fix us supper."

"Mighty kind of you, Iris."

When Pel arrived, the cops were waiting. It had only taken me a minute to call them.

He confessed before they even read him his rights. "I'm doing the Lord's work. Weren't no sin in it."

"Right, buddy, save it for the judge."

They cuffed Pel, pushed him into the back of a battered black-and-white patrol car.

Cop in charge hitched up his britches, looked around my yard. "See you got yourself a honeycrisp here, ma'am. That tree don't never normally grow round these parts. It's a cold, cold-natured apple, needs a place with plenty of ice." He spit on the crabgrass.

"Luckadoo Landscaping," I said. "I'm my daddy's daughter."

After they took Pel away I walked into the backyard shed, took a seat among evil-eyed critters with big bellies and pointy heads, listening to the wooden silence of left-behind trolls. Slowly there grew inside me a great green envy for those with relics of hope.

MARY ALICE DIXON grew up in Carolina red clay mixed with Appalachian coal dust. She has worked as a professor of architectural history and as a popcorn counter waitress, though not at the same time. Mary Alice is a Pushcart nominee, Pinesong Award winner, finalist for the Doris Betts Fiction Prize, and nominee for Best Small Fiction. Her work has appeared in dozens of publications, including *Kakalak*, *Main Street Rag*, *moonShine review*, *Northern Appalachia Review*, *The Petigru Review*, *The RavensPerch*, and four anthologies from Daniel Boone Footsteps Press. Mary Alice lives in Charlotte, NC where she sometimes speaks with the ghosts of her dead cats Thomas Merton and Alice B. Toklas.

The Woman, Being Deceived
Karen Sleeth

Years of weathered abuse deformed the ashen and desolate gray porch boards and caused them to cup and curve. In addition to a feeble bench and methodically stacked woodpile, the porch bore a rusty hand pump. This is where Dory headed as she stepped into the sharp bitterness of the January morning, letting the outer screen door slam behind her.

A pair of fingerless gloves, tattered sweater, and a silk scarf were her only protection from the cold. She had a coat, a heavy coat. Bobby Ray had given it to her for Christmas.

"Please wear it, Mom," he had begged. But it would be too easy.

Dory began the rhythmic pumping of the frozen metal handle that forced the water up feet of pipe, splashing into her bucket. As she pumped, she watched the farm waking with the rising sun, the sight she had viewed daily for the past forty years. The chickens fussing and pecking over the feed Claude had strewn in their yard. The soft mooing and stamping of the cattle in the barn and Claude's voice soothing them. The comforting sights and sounds that were marred by the dreaded insistence she knew would soon begin.

"Why do you do it, Gramma?" Bobby Jr. had pleaded.

"I have to," she had replied, but had no response to his persistent *why* and averted eyes.

After that, she avoided getting water when his bus came. She knew it embarrassed him. It shamed her too, but that was her penance, not his.

The voice of the water spilled over the lip of the bucket and demanded she begin. She exhaled, carried the pail down the steps, and placed it exactly three inches from the first stepping-stone.

"Three inches for three sins," she began, repeating after the echo in her head. Her arms lifted automatically upward and began the slow circular motion that then swept through her torso.

"One-two-three, four-five-six, seven," she said. The echo said, *It is finished.* Her arms fell, pinned hard to her side, just as the long-departed Reverend Hadley had held her as a young teen. His face loomed, his hot breath assaulting, the cold blue eyes drawing closer and closer.

The tingling began once again. First in the tips of her toes and then it crept up her legs, leaving her body jolting as if electrified.

Step two, he said and she grabbed the bucket and ran several feet, stopping short.

The walk of penance, he said. She resolutely placed her feet into the well-worn foot holes, which formed a pattern in the yard. After each step he repeated the verses he had used on that day. The day he said he would bring her closer to God.

Let the woman learn in silence with all submission. Dory turned several times and then took another step.

But I suffer a woman not to usurp authority over the man, but be in silence. The words reverberated through her head as she crouched to the ground.

The woman, being deceived, was in transgression. As if shocked, she bolted upright.

After several more squats, jumps, and turns she pivoted, brushed her graying hair back and retraced her steps through the yard. She lifted the partially full bucket and continued up the stairs, justified for a time.

The main room of their small house served as kitchen, dining, and living room. Dory carried the bucket directly to the stove where she poured water into the coffee pot. A small stream spilled, hissing and dancing on the surface until it melted into steam. From the crate behind the range, she took a piece of wood and poked it into the firebox. The flames thrust from the opening, grasping for her hand and she slammed the lid. The fire howled like an animal caught in a trap, then calmed to a crackle. Removing her gloves and scarf, she draped them over the gray coat hanging behind the door and returned to the stove. Dory held her hands out to capture the heat waves climbing to the ceiling. She breathed in the smokey fragrance and sighed.

On the far wall Claude had nailed the calendar with "Church of the Redeemer - 1959" printed as the heading. It had little months that tore off the bottom and at the top, the one same picture remained all year long. She scowled. Claude had picked up this copy at the feed store and it had been hanging there two weeks already. She had cried when she first saw it. She didn't know why. The colors, unnaturally bright, hadn't been lined up quite right when the calendar was printed, and Dory got dizzy when she looked closely. The picture of Jesus, his lips outlined in blue, gazed down at a woman curled up at his feet. She seemed frightened and the caption read, *Neither do I condemn thee. Go and sin no more.*

When she was a child, Dory's Sunday School teacher had told the story of how the woman had been caught in adultery, and though everyone wanted to kill her, Jesus had convinced them to leave her alone.

Then Jesus had just plain forgiven her.

What had happened to the woman afterward—had she forgiven herself? No one ever talked about that. If she had, the townsfolk probably pecked her to death when Jesus left, calling her names, ridiculing her, avoiding her, and not letting her forget. If she had picked up the phone, she probably would have heard them talking about her, too.

Claude had called her silly to let a calendar fret her, but she just couldn't get out of her mind the picture of the woman crouching at Jesus' feet.

Claude had said the woman wasn't scared, just grateful not to be killed. But Dory couldn't understand how the woman could be grateful, being left to face her guilt day after day. Claude had called her silly again, hadn't Jesus given her forgiveness, he said? But it didn't make sense to Dory. A one-time forgiveness didn't take care of everyday guilt, the kind that demanded payment with every breath, the kind she felt every time she looked into the cool blue of Bobby Ray's eyes.

That night when Claude's breathing sounded like the old pump, she was drawn into the kitchen to see if the woman was still crouched at Jesus' feet. She hoped the woman had walked away. But in the bottom right corner of the page, there she sat while Jesus stood, handing out forgiveness, towering over her curled figure. Dory studied the woman. She was scrunched down like she wished she were smaller, her eyes focused on Jesus' feet. Would she change with the descending pardon? Would she get bigger or stand tall? At one point there might have been a change, a light started to shine, but it was just the glare of the rising sun on the shiny paper.

In the morning Dory dressed, and began the vital ritual to fill the bucket. She finished each step with practiced precision, but the voice was not satisfied long. Taking each log off the woodpile she re-stacked it, with the ends perfectly lined-up, until her hands and legs were red and numb with cold. She fed Claude breakfast and washed and dried every dish three times, then returned to observe the picture.

"My God, Dory! Sit down. Stop standing there clutching your hands and weaving in circles," Claude said, jarring her attention from the calendar. She hadn't heard him come in. He peeled off hat, scarf, gloves, coat, and sweater. His dry hands scraped like corncobs as he rubbed them.

"Here, get me a cup of coffee," he said, handing her the huge pink and white cup he had bought at a novelty shop.

"Doc Morgan told you to stop drinking coffee." She filled the bowl-sized cup anyway.

Claude chuckled. "He said I could have one cup a day."

"He meant a regular cup." But Claude insisted on drinking his coffee from this tureen, as if he was somehow outsmarting the doctor.

"He never said nothing about the size. Quit your nagging." Claude sat and opened the paper to the funnies.

"You ought to do what he says, Claude."

"All right, all right, after this cup." Claude's voice trailed off and he mouthed the words in the comics. He turned the page and looked up at Dory.

"You need anything in town? I got to get a new handle for the axe. The head came flying off and darn near took mine with it." He put down the paper and caressed the big cup.

Dory slowly shook her head. "It's the Sabbath, Claude. You know I don't hold with buying and selling on—"

"Since when is Friday the Sabbath, Dory?" He lifted the cup to his mouth.

"Jesus started on Friday and I reckon what Jesus did ain't too good for me."

"That's funny. His forgiveness ain't good enough for you." Claude put down the cup and went back to mouthing the funnies. Dory glanced at him and then the calendar and at Jesus forgiving the crumpled-up woman. The blue outline of his lips was barely visible.

"Remember the Sabbath day to keep it holy. That's what the Good Book says," her voice was shaking.

Claude dropped the paper on the table. "I don't mind keeping a day holy, Dory. You just pick the day and I'll abide by it."

"Suppose I pick the wrong one?" she said, her voice rising. "I'm not about to be kept out of Glory because I chose the wrong day!"

Claude shook his head.

"I know it's somewhere on the weekend. If I start Friday and end Tuesday morning, I'm sure to get it," she said.

The blue lips were saying something, but Dory couldn't understand.

"I won't be kept out for the wrong day," she shouted, rubbing and twisting her hands. The blue lips moved--trying to tell her something. She struggled to hear the whisper. It came from the water on the stove and not the lips, more like a hiss than a whisper. She strained her attention to the voice of the water.

Keep the S-S-Sabbath, it said. She tried to respond, but her lips would not move. Every other noise died to Dory's ear, only the voice of the water remained. Claude got up from the table. His lips moved close to her face, but the warning of the water drowned him out. She tried to lift her hands and cover her ears, but her arms were pinned down. The water grew louder.

Claude went out and left her alone with the calendar and the shouting from the water.

The water's demands to keep the sabbath were now answered by the reminder that *the woman, being deceived, was in transgression.* Dory wanted to scream, clamp her hands over her ears, run from the room but she stood paralyzed, unable to silence the voices. She had a dry bitter taste in her mouth and she longed for quiet and a sip of cool water.

Claude came back into the kitchen with Bobby Ray and other people. They moved through the room, staring into her face and shining lights into her eyes, but all she could hear was the hissing and howling voices in her head. After they lifted her and strapped her onto the stretcher, Bobby Ray placed a gray coat over her shivering body. His face loomed over her, his cold blue eyes drawing closer and closer.

"The woman, being deceived, was in transgression," she shouted over and over. Reverend Hadley drew his face quickly away.

When they opened the door to take her out, the wind lifted the calendar off the wall. *Neither do I condemn thee* flutter upward and then drifted down, out the door. The calendar disappeared between the boards of the porch floor as the stretcher bumped over the curved boards, down the steps and over the deeply worn foot path in the yard.

Karen Sleeth earned a BA in English Literature from UNC-CH. She receives an MFA in Creative Writing from Lindenwood University in May 2023. Karen's work has appeared or is forthcoming in *The Main Street Rag, Potato Soup Journal, 2022 Best of Potato Soup Journal, Lost and Found – 2023 Personal Story Publishing Project*, and others.

ACKNOWLEDGMENTS

THIS PROJECT HAS BEEN A LONG PROCESS, and I would like to thank Kimberly Verhines, director of the SFA Press, for being a fantastic guide from start to finish. Working with her for the past two years has been such a fruitful experience, and I am so grateful to have been part of the SFA Publishing program. Her knowledge and expertise is unmatched, and I am incredibly blessed to have her as a mentor.

I would also like to thank the "Publishing Puff Girls," Mallory LeCroy and Katt Noble, who worked closely by my side and watched the creation of this anthology from the beginning. Your input was, and always will be, highly valuable, and I thank you for being my wing-women. Of course, all the members of our Publishing program have seen and critiqued this anthology at some point in the process, whether it be the website, a flyer, or even the cover, and I thank you all, too.

I would also like to thank Dr. Sue Whatley and Kim Bradley for being early readers and for providing blurbs to include with the book. I admire the contributions you have both made to the study and genre of Southern Gothic, and I appreciate the time you have offered to make this book better. And, of course, a huge thanks to Joe R. Lansdale for writing the foreword. This was an idea I had at the very beginning of this project, and I am so honored that you were able to contribute.

Additionally, I must thank all the writers who submitted to this anthology, and especially to the ones who were selected as contributors. Thank you all for your patience and your trust in this process.

Of course, there are tons of people in the background who have made this book possible, and they probably don't even know. I would like to thank my undergraduate professors, especially Dr. Sara Henning, who helped me plan this anthology in its earliest stages, and Dr. John McDermott and Andrew Brininstool, who taught my fiction workshops and craft-based classes. Through those classes, your instruction, and your assigned readings, I developed an eye, or at least a love, for short stories that I hope shines through in this collection.

And finally, what would an acknowledgments page be with out a shout-out to my family? I am so grateful to my parents, sisters, and extended family members and friends who have been my cheerleaders throughout my time with the SFA Press. You are all truly the best.

About the Editor

MEREDITH JANNING serves as an editorial assistant for the Stephen F. Austin State University Press. In 2023, she earned her MA in Publishing and holds a BA in Mass Communication (Journalism) with a minor in Creative Writing, both from SFA. Meredith is passionate about sharing literature—she especially loves the work of Flannery O'Connor—and this anthology is a product of that love.